Grande Dames AND A Vegas Heist

MJ MILLER

For Eric, 6 down 94 to go

TRADEMARK ACKNOWLEDGEMENTS

- Sherlock - *Conan Doyle Estate Ltd owns the trademark for the name Sherlock (Holmes)*
- Watson - *Conan Doyle Estate Ltd owns the trademark for the name Watson*
- MacGyver - *registered trademark of Auras Unlimited Productions, Inc*
- Jon Bon Jovi - *trademark owned by Bon Jovi Productions, Inc*
- Inspector Clouseau - *rights owned by Metro-Goldwyn-Mayer*
- Agent Mulder - *rights owned by Fox/20th Century Studios*
- Curious George - *copyrighted and trademarked by Houghton Mifflin Harcourt Publishing Company*
- Google - *registered trademark owned by Google LLC, under parent company Alphabet, Inc*
- Lone Ranger - *name and show rights owned by NBC Universal*
- Kemosabe - *rights owned by NBCUniversal*
- BBC Pride and Prejudice - *production owned by British Broadcasting Corporation*
- *Jane Austen - public domain*
- Indiana Jones - *trademark owned by Lucasfilm Ltd LLC*
- James Bond 007 - *trademark owned by DANJAQ LLC*
- Flash - *trademark owned by DC Comics*

- Bruno Mars - *trademark owned by Mars Force Trademarks, LLC*
- Magnum - *registered trademark for Universal City Studios LLC*
- Amazon - *trademark owned by Amazon Technologies, Inc*
- Hallmark - *trademark owned by Crown Media United States, LLC, which runs Hallmark Cards Inc, Hallmark Licensing LLC, hallmark.com*
- Jane Austen - *public domain*
- Count Dracula - *public domain*
- *Frankenstein – public domain*
- Charlie's Angels - registered trademark of Columbia Pictures Industries Inc
- Scarface - *trademark owned by Universal Pictures and Universal City Studios LLC*
- Bridget Jones - *copyright Helen Fielding*
- Mark Darcy - *copyright Helen Fielding*
- Marvel - *The Walt Disney Company owns the Marvel Entertainment brand but doesn't own rights for all characters; Marvel Characters Inc has trademarks for lots of products*
- Scarlett O'Hara - *registered trademark for film products and characters owned by Turner Entertainment Co*
- Inspector Gadget - *registered trademark of Cookie Jar Entertainment Inc, rights owned by DHX Media?*
- Scooby Doo - *copyright and registered trademark of Hanna-Barbera Productions Inc*
- House Hunters - *registered trademark owned by Scripps Networks, LLC*
- Groucho - *registered trademark of Groucho Marx Productions*

- Harpo - *registered trademark of Groucho Marx Productions*
- Columbo - *registered trademark of Universal City Studios, LLC*
- eBay - *trademark owned by EBAY Inc*
- HGTV - *registered trademark of Scripps Networks, LLC*
- The Travel Channel - *copyright owned by Disney, trademark owned by The Travel Channel LLC*
- Agent 99 *(Get Smart, CBS Media Ventures)*
- Name That Tune *– NBC Radio*
- Bluetooth - *registered trademarks owned by Bluetooth SIG, Inc.*
- Jeep *– brand name of FCA US LLC.*
- CSI - *CBS*
- *Instagram*
- *Facebook*
- *Twitter*
- *Melissa Etheridge- Celebrity*
- Clue *– Copyrighted by Hasbro*
- Ken Doll. *Mattel Inc.*

CHAPTER ONE

MUSCLES BURNING, LEGS SCREAMING, BACK ACHING, I BARELY HEARD the spring thunderstorm raging outside. Instead, I ambitiously attempted a Lord of The Fishes yoga pose while simultaneously swearing and admiring the aging but agile video instructor for her effortless performance.

Concentrating so hard, I doubted anything could tear me from my mandate to beat my body into submission, but that was when the familiar ringtone I'd assigned to my twin sister ripped me from near perfection. Groaning, I considered ignoring her but then realized that would be an invitation to disaster, so I undid my pretzel-like pose and grabbed my phone.

"Who died?" I asked before huffing out a frustrated but semi-relieved breath.

"Pippa, I've got a fabulous idea!"

Please, god, no.

"What might that be, Babs?"

"A yard sale."

"You just donated half your wardrobe and a basement full of boxes to the community center. What's left to sell, your organs?"

"Don't be silly. Since Mother and Father are off to the cabin for their version of spring break, we can finally tidy up her place." Babs, short for Barbara, always referred to our mom as Mother. Dad as Father. It was some sort of affectation she'd picked up during high school, which she'd begun referring to as finishing school.

My mother's house was indeed filled with clutter. I didn't mind, but it annoyed my sister, who had a deep and abiding obsession with organization. It bugged my dad too, so much so he'd actually moved next door.

My mother and father adored each other but were unable to live in the same house. They did, however, share meals, work together, and go out together, and while I didn't like to imagine this, they probably still enjoyed each other.

All that aside, cluttered as my mother's house was, I didn't think it had reached the level that would find a reality TV psychologist knocking at the door accompanied by those big-ass haul-away trucks and guys in hazmat suits—not yet, anyway.

"Do you have a death wish? Mom likes her house as it is. Just leave it alone."

"I can't leave it. We'll never be able to sell that house if we don't get it organized and spiffy."

"Her house isn't for sale, and I'm pretty sure she's not intending to move."

"Yes, but someday she will. Or she'll die. And then we'll have to sell it."

I thought about hanging up and going back to my fish yoga, but the masochist in me kept me on the line. "Mom doesn't want you to sell all her worldly goods out from under her. I highly recommend you move on to your next fabulous idea. And to be clear, I want no part of this one, understand?"

I knew full well Babs didn't understand at all. It wasn't that she was dim-witted, quite the contrary—she just didn't consider consequences applied to her.

I desperately hoped for some divine intervention at that point. Beyond a doubt, Mom would be furious, not just with Babs, but with me. As twins, Babs and I shared everything, including the blame.

Sisters are sisters for life. You take care of each other. That was something my mother liked to remind me of when I dared to complain, but she was an only child. She had *no* idea.

However, I had a terrifying premonition that things were about to go sideways.

I should have stayed far, far, away from Bab's sellathon, which she'd miraculously put together for the following weekend. As it turned out, it was a glorious sunny Saturday morning, and I couldn't resist stopping by just to see what was happening. As I scoped out the neat and festive tables on which she'd laid out Mom's treasures, I remembered my mom mentioning that she'd scored an incredible Navajo rug at a local crafts show. Thinking I could nab it for myself before Babs sold it, I went inside and did a thorough search. I'd nearly given up when I finally spotted the rug rolled up on a shelf in my mom's hall closet stuck behind several layers of boxes—which I had to pull down and place on the floor. Delighted at unearthing my prize, I was about to put the boxes back when someone began banging around downstairs. Assuming it was Babs, I hauled the rug back to my car and slipped away, full of glee and without a thought to any kind of impending disaster.

Babs was quite holier-than-thou when she called later that night.

"Pip, I have to say, I've never seen Mother's house looking

so lovely. The garbage is finally gone, and we made quite a tidy sum."

I swore softly to myself before responding. I hadn't wanted to hear that Bab's fabulous idea had been a success. "Well, congratulations, and all credit to you. Just make sure you take *all* the credit for selling Mom's stuff." I may have sounded tense, but that was because keeping Babs in check and minding our family antique shop by myself was wearing me thin.

I still expected some fallout when our parents returned, but that was a week away, so I wasn't expecting an ominous text from Babs mere hours after that first jubilant phone call.

Babs: Emergency. Mother's house. NOW!

There was no point in calling or texting her back because she wouldn't respond. Babs tended to issue commands and expected me to obey without question. I probably encouraged her by always doing exactly what she wanted when I should just ignore her. In this case, if it were truly an emergency, she would have called her devoted husband, Tom. He was always calm and rational in a crisis, so there wasn't a true emergency, just Babs wanting attention as usual. Tom also may have been at home with Leah, their three-year-old daughter. I caved and headed to Mom's place, which was a short distance across town. Luckland wasn't large by any means. A small town that still retained its charming historic downtown, all eight blocks or so of it, Luckland met our tight-knit community's needs outside Denver without the cookie-cutter suburban feel.

As I drove, I tried to figure out what the "emergency" was. Maybe the sprayer hose in the sink went on a wild air dance and flooded the kitchen. Maybe Babs broke that creepy skeleton floor lamp in the foyer. Maybe she crawled out of the attic window to wipe off a smudge, locked herself out, and was hanging on a ledge... No such luck. Babs sat on the front step of

Mom's slightly worn three-story Victorian, head in her hands and looking quite forlorn.

Babs and I were as fraternal as twins could be—different as night and day and as sugar and spice. Babs was all sugar with the blonde hair and blue eyes from our mother. I was the spice, and I got the red hair and green eyes from Dad's side. I must have had his sense of humor too because Babs and Mom didn't seem to have one. Or if they did, it was well hidden.

I sat next to her. "Okay, Babs, spill it."

She lifted her head slowly and looked at me, her large blue eyes filled with tears, which I suspected might be a ploy. Babs had learned early on that tears could bend the will of others. I was a foot stomper, which wasn't quite as effective.

"They're gone, Pippa," she said ever so softly.

"What's gone?"

"They're all gone." She shook her head.

"What, Babs? What's gone?" My muscles began to tense—the way they did whenever she played the tragedy card when there wasn't an actual tragedy.

She fluttered her hands nervously and continued to shake her head. "Not *what*, Pip, *who*."

"Who? All right then, who's gone?"

"Uncle Ernie, for one. And Aunt Lucy too." She gave a little sniffle and dabbed at her eyes.

I tried to sort through her nonsensical response. "Of course, they're gone. They've always been gone. It's what happens to dead people."

My attitude must have riled her up at that point because she dropped the pretense of being overwrought.

"Don't be an idiot, Pip. I know they're *deceased*. But now they're truly gone."

"Babs, you haven't been hitting Mom's secret stash, have you?"

She looked at me as if I'd suddenly sprouted a second head. "I mean, their boxes are gone. You know, in the closet. They're gone."

"Oh. Well, now, that's a bit of a snafu." *More like an apocalyptic catastrophe.* "How did they end up gone?"

"Haven't you been paying attention? We sold them!" Babs sighed overdramatically.

I winced. My mom had *lovingly* labeled each shoebox with a name and a year. Whether that was their birth, death, or anniversary, who knew? What I did know, or what my mom eventually told me, was that they were literally my mother's aunts, uncles, and parents.

Growing up, I was sure each box held cherished mementos and memorabilia, like an amethyst brooch in Aunt Lucy's box, perhaps given to her by a long-ago beau, or a letter expressing the undying and desperate love of a soldier during the Great War, maybe a postcard sent from one of her many excursions to far off exotic destinations. In Uncle Ernie's box, there might have been an autographed baseball from Babe Ruth, possibly an old pocket watch, or even a photograph of his wedding day.

Except this was the O'Leary family, not a *normal* family by any stretch. On my sixteenth birthday, when I had decided I was entitled to view the contents, my mother informed me that the boxes contained *cremains*. Cremated cadavers. Leftover bits and pieces of the Murphy dynasty.

I'd never been to any of their funerals or memorials—not even a cocktail reception celebrating their demise. With a name like O'Leary, I should have attended at least one or two old-fashioned Irish wakes. But no. Kate O'Leary, aka Mom, didn't believe anyone should stand around moping when someone was gone. She always said to appreciate them while they were here, and that was enough.

While my mother was entirely at ease merely waving

goodbye to the souls of the dearly departed, she insisted on keeping everything else. Packrat didn't even begin to tell her story. Figuring out my mother had always been my life's biggest mystery, but that was neither here nor there. Thanks to my sister and those damn boxes, we faced a crisis of gargantuan proportions. What was more, though I had nothing to do with it, I was still going to cop some of the blame.

As I searched in my bag for a quasi-clean tissue for Babs, whose mascara was running a marathon at that point, I wondered how she could have sold the boxes. That was when it hit me. My planned speech at denying any involvement came to a blazing halt as I realized, in some abstract fashion, I might have had something to do with this fiasco. The boxes I'd left on the floor were shoeboxes—*those* shoeboxes, the ones filled with our family's remains.

As we sat on the steps, side by side, Babs rambled about how she'd enlisted the boys next door to be her helpers. I'd seen them bouncing around but hadn't paid them any attention. I surmised from Babs's tale of woe that the helpers had sealed up the boxes, placed them on the table in the garage, stuck a price tag of five dollars on each one, and wrote "Surprise Buy."

"Wait, why would you even let them sell those boxes?"

"They weren't supposed to sell *those* boxes, they were supposed to sell the other boxes. I told them to grab the boxes in the hallway."

I remembered the other pile of boxes in the hall closet and guessed that was where the mix-up happened. That was my moment to tell her I was the one who'd left the shoeboxes on the floor. Instead, I decided to wait for a more...appropriate time. "So, they grabbed the wrong boxes?"

"Clearly." Her tone was somewhat haughty. It seemed as if she'd decided on whom to lay the blame.

I was fully aware how bargain hunters couldn't resist a

temptation. I could imagine a seasoned yard sale vet picking up a box, giving it a shake, and listening for tell-tale sounds that might indicate hidden treasure. I could almost see the gleam in their eyes as they bargained the price down to two dollars before happily running off with their find, only to get home, open it, and discover that Aunt Lucy meant just that—Lucy in the box, sans diamonds.

"Look, Babs, maybe the buyers will return them. Once they see what's inside," I said, trying to impart a bit of hope.

"No, no, they won't, Pip. They'll throw them away. That's what I would do. I mean, ew, boxes of ashes?"

I could see my squeamish sister's point. "Well then, there's not much to do except tell Mom that the *dearly* have finally *departed* and hope she lets you live." I chuckled a bit at my twisted sense of humor, hoping she'd relax. I wasn't having much luck in that department, either.

"Are you crazy, she's going to kill me." Babs gave me another of her tearful doe-eyed looks.

As much as I enjoyed watching her squirm, I knew if anyone ended up groveling for mercy, it would be me. Babs was notorious for seemingly getting away with everything and anything. Me? I seemed to perpetually suffer the consequences.

CHAPTER TWO

"You did what?" My mother's face had a slightly contorted expression. The *angry mom about to blow* look. I was surprised she'd waited so long to confront us. She had returned Sunday night to her newly cleaned-out abode, then headed over to Dad's to vent before waiting a full twelve hours to drag us over here for the reckoning.

I turned to Babs, waiting for her to cleverly deflect that one.

"We had a yard sale, Mother. One that earned you over five hundred dollars, I might add." Babs really needed to learn how to control her smugness. She then spun around, waving her arms. "Look at how fabulous this place looks! No more junkyard ambience."

I debated whether to continue to let her dig her grave or come to her rescue. I decided to come to her rescue. "Mom, I think what Babs is trying to say is she thought she was being helpful by organizing and perhaps thinning out your collection of...things." Looking around, I realized Babs must have exercised immeasurable control because our mom's furniture was still intact. I had to admit, the house did look exceptionally tidy.

"Girls, I just give up. What am I going to do with you? You're grown women, yet I can't leave you alone for a minute. For god's sake, what were you thinking?" My mother circled around us like a bird of prey with hands clasped behind her. Her short blonde hair bobbed as she paced.

"Wasn't my idea, Mom," I answered, albeit pointlessly. Mom was going to blame me the same as Babs.

"And then you do nothing? Just wait for me to come back and make it better?" She blew out the last words in a rush. "My Uncle Ernie. Honestly, girls! He paid for your college education and then some!" Her words seemed to have the desired effect of inducing more guilt. In retrospect, I probably should have stopped Babs from having the sale, or perhaps left the rug alone. At the very least, I should have put the boxes back. Unfortunately, I didn't, and I still hadn't come clean to Babs about my involvement.

"Well. We're going to need help on this," my mother said with some finality. "We better call for reinforcements."

Babs and I looked at each other in horror. This was not good. Whenever my mother referred to reinforcements, she meant her friends. Her lifelong besties—Matilda, Hope, and Prudence. The kind of friends that took "butting in" to a whole new level. Yeah, not good.

It was no surprise when my mother summoned us two days later to her ad-hoc Luckland Ladies' Auxiliary luncheon to sort out our mess. We sat around my mother's ancient but sturdy patio table—the big round glass kind with the umbrella going straight up the middle.

Matilda, tall, lithe, and striking, had dressed in her most fashionable muumuu, a vibrant red, flowing Hawaiian-styled dress, which had something to do with entering a new phase in her life. She'd tossed out her razors, stopped coloring her hair, and decided she was going to "let me be me" in her own way. Next to Matilda sat Hope, her nails perfectly manicured, her back straight, and her tiny frame primly perched on her chair. She'd coiffed her recently colored golden-brown hair into a bun and wore an expectant expression. Hope always seemed to believe intrigue was just around the corner.

Then there was Prudence. Her heavy mane of auburn hair fell in waves about her shoulders. Petite in stature but curvy enough, as she liked to say, she was perpetually about two shots of tequila away from causing a ruckus. Her day usually started with mimosas and ended with whiskey, with maybe a nice bottle of Chardonnay in between, and a few kamikazes on the weekends. Nevertheless, age had done nothing to quell Pru's beauty—her free spirit, I was sure, contributed.

After a good twenty minutes of chitchat, the subject turned to current events. My mother cleared her throat, and everyone focused on her.

"Well, I suppose you are all wondering why we're here. Pippa? Care to explain?"

"Hard pass," I politely replied, wondering what she'd said to her friends about Babs's little misadventure. Or even if Mom had said anything at all.

"Very well. Barbara, if you'll do the honors?"

"Oh, Mother, for goodness' sake." Babs turned to face the women and gave them a substantially abridged version. "My mother is just a little concerned because, during the recent, highly successful, I might add, yard sale, a few boxes went missing."

"Tell them which boxes," my mother said.

"Shoeboxes. Somebody appears to have accidentally purchased Aunt Lucy instead of Jimmy Choo." Babs smiled, and

I wondered how long it took her to come up with that clever quip.

"*The* boxes?" Pru asked.

"Yes," my mother said, her tone pinched.

"Oh."

The atmosphere in the room suddenly changed from friendly to strained. A glance at the ladies revealed mutual deer-in-headlights expressions—which I thought strange as these ladies were generally unflappable.

After a moment of silence, Matilda cleared her throat. "No need to panic, Kate. We just need to get them back, and all will be well."

"How? My girls don't know who bought them, and I don't know where to start looking." She shook her head, her frustration mounting. "You know what? We need a PI."

"Seriously, Mom? You want to call a private investigator and tell them to find your shoeboxes filled with ashes?" That bordered on lunacy, and by the look on Babs's face, she thought so too.

"I think that's a great idea, and don't you worry," Matilda said. "I know just the guy for the job."

CHAPTER THREE

Several days after the ladies' odd reaction to the missing shoeboxes, my mom ushered the man who was supposed to find them into her living room. "Devon, my dear, sit, sit. What can I get you?"

"I'm good. No need to put yourself out," he said as he gracefully dropped into the comfy recliner directly opposite Babs and me.

I tried not to stare. When Matilda said she had the perfect guy for the job, I figured she knew someone in Denver who may or may not have a license to investigate. I was expecting one of her eccentric friends or even a cigar-smoking gray-haired potbellied mall security cop. What I didn't expect was Matilda's pigtail-pulling nephew.

Growing up, he was one of those children from hell I'd tried my best to avoid, so when he sauntered into my mother's living room—six feet and some odd inches, maybe two hundred pounds, all muscle, piercing greenish-blue eyes, and a killer smile, I was floored.

I'd never in my wildest dreams imagined he'd grow up to be

007. Stuffy lawyer maybe, mad scientist, corporate raider, embezzler... But this? No.

We hadn't seen him since Babs's wedding, and Devon at twenty-two couldn't hold a candle to Devon at thirty. Something about those intervening years seemed to have worn awfully well on him. Matilda would occasionally talk about him. *Devon has a new position. Devon is dating a model. Devon is off traveling again.* I hadn't really cared. I might have been a little curious as we never saw him, but overall, Devon had become a bit of a mystery.

"Hello, Barbara," he said with a smile as he nodded politely at Babs. "Hey, Red." He grinned, knowing I absolutely detested that nickname. Then he winked. Devon Marks winked at me. Right then and there, I knew trouble had arrived.

While waiting for the Luckland Ladies brigade to arrive, it became a bit too quiet for my liking. As I wasn't one for awkward silences, I dove right in. "So, Devon, what brings you back to Luckland?" Maybe I was wrong, and he *wasn't* a PI. A girl could hope.

"Not sure, Pippa, that's what I'm here to find out."

"You don't know why you're here? That seems a little odd." Babs studied his expression as if trying to determine how much he knew.

"Aunt Tillie called and said I needed to come home. That it was an emergency. That's all," he said. "Maybe you two could fill me in?" He raised his eyebrows as if silently asking us to fess up. As if that was going to happen. Thankfully, Matilda, Prudence, and Hope marched in like the grande dames they were.

Devon stood, greeted his aunt with a great big bear hug, and offered the same to the others. Like Babs and me, as a child, Devon was at the receiving end of the ladies' group maternal ministering. In his case, however, it was far more dramatic. He was the unfortunate victim of a very sad tale. As the story went, his saintly parents had been in the diplomatic corps in the Congo. Kidnapped by rebels, no one ever saw his parents again. Matilda raised Devon as if he were her own.

As I continued to stare at him, I wondered why he hadn't come *with* Matilda. I mean, I would have thought he'd have gone to her house the minute he got into town then accompanied her here. I also wondered what it was about him that had my pulse racing and why I couldn't help but notice the length of his lashes or the way his mouth curved into a smile sometimes... I mean, this was Devon, but he was fascinating in ways I'd never imagined. Could it be because there weren't a lot of options in Luckland when single? And smoking hot options? Well, they were non-existent.

While my mind wandered into places it had no business going, my mom and her pals settled on the big, comfy sofa. Devon also sat back down, then swung one long, lean leg over the other before he clasped his hands together, interlocking his fingers like a principal when they were about to ream someone for something. I knew that feeling well.

"Okay, ladies, I'm here. What's the emergency? And why is it the twins couldn't handle it?"

"Just to verify, Devon, I take it you're a Private Investigator." Babs *had* to state the obvious.

"In a manner of speaking," he said.

"Exactly what manner of speaking is that, Devon?" Me? I just *had* to push his buttons. At least I was getting back into my groove; anything to quash my strange reaction to him.

He seemed to ignore my attempt at being a wiseass, which was unusual for him. I remembered a time when he would have reacted with some holier-than-thou response.

"Look, I'm here. You're all here. Let's get to it, shall we? What's going on, Pip?"

Ah, yes, there was the Devon I knew. Just a little impatient and abrupt.

Matilda cleared her throat, presumably because she knew I had a bit of a fiery temper. My dad blamed it on my Irish heritage, while I figured it was due to my being a redhead. Regardless, my temper was something Devon had managed to ignite since we were small.

"Devon, it appears that Barbara held a yard sale, during which a few things disappeared from Kate's house that we need to get back."

"I'm sorry, Aunt Tillie, but that's your emergency?"

"Yes. I'm afraid the boxes that disappeared were quite important. The contents were priceless."

"Oh, well, in *that* case."

"No need to be snippy, Devon," I said, calling him out on it because I knew nobody else would dare, especially Matilda—she thought the sun shone from his ass.

"Look, Red, if they're that important, why did you sell them?"

"For the record, Harpo, *I* did not, technically, sell them," I replied.

My mother took the opportunity to do her annoying hand clap, where she stood, clapped, and called everyone to attention as if she were back in the classroom. She was not a typical teacher, however. She taught drama in Adult Ed.

"Children, behave. Now, Devon, there were six boxes in my closet where I kept some of the family remains. Those are the boxes. Obviously, we need to get them back. You will help, won't you?"

Devon had no choice. I think we all knew that.

He sighed, then turned on his fifty-million-watt smile at my mother. "Sure, Kate. I'll see what I can do. But I'll need some help."

I honestly wasn't sure where that would lead, but considering how we got into this mess, I was most definitely offering up Babs as the volunteer.

"I'm sure Barbara would love to help you, Devon." I smiled at him, sweetly, of course.

Fluttering her hands just like Mom, Babs immediately went into excuse mode. "I have a strict schedule to keep with Leah, and I'm afraid any deviation just throws things off." Babs turned her blue eyes on Devon and smiled. "Motherhood," she said with a shrug.

"So, all hell will break loose if you don't get to roll out of bed at ten? Why does a three-year-old dictate your life anyway?" It annoyed me to no end when she used the motherhood line.

"It's very important to keep my word, and we have plans already."

"I'm sure you do. Let me guess, a playdate? Perhaps followed by a pedicure?"

Babs didn't work outside the home. She didn't work *inside* the home. She lived a comfortable, somewhat entitled life and saw no need to earn an income because money wasn't an issue. Tom, my brother-in-law, made sure of that. Babs could certainly help Devon. She just wouldn't.

"Pip, socialization for a three-year-old is critical, and as for the pedicure, you do realize that toenail trauma can cause a hematoma, don't you? This is your niece we're talking about."

Devon seemed unperturbed by our bickering. He focused those aquamarine eyes on me, tipped his head in a way that did not bode well, then smiled. I knew right then I was in big trouble. He was up to something, and it wouldn't end well. For me.

"No worries, Babs." He said this while his gaze remained locked on mine. "Pippa will be happy to help, won't you, Pippa? And bring that camera you've always got hanging around your neck, would you? Let's you and I reconvene at the café, say seven hundred hours, tomorrow?"

Reconvene? Seven hundred hours? He must be jet-lagged. I had no idea where he'd flown in from, but I was ready for him to flap his little wings and fly on out. However, I wouldn't give him the satisfaction of showing him just what I thought of his *reconvening*. "By café, you mean the Blue Sky, I assume?"

"Where else?" He smiled, and I noticed how his eyes crinkled. I should've focused on coming up with an excuse, but before I had a chance to say anything, everyone stood and chattered excitedly about the fact that Devon was here, Devon would take charge, and Devon would get it all fixed.

"Excuse me," I said politely, trying to get everyone's attention. Nothing. I tried three times, but after no response, I got fed up. So, with two fingers in my mouth, I let off a shrieking whistle. That did it.

"Pippa!" my mother exclaimed, appalled.

"Sorry, but if anyone cares to ask, I have a current project I'm working on. I'd planned a hike tomorrow to get a few shots of the spring wildflower bloom. The *Nature's Future* project? Ring a bell here?" They all knew I'd scored a chance at a potential assignment from one of Colorado's most prominent environmental groups. It could land me my dream job and propel my blog into the stratosphere. Maybe stratosphere was a stretch, but I did have aspirations.

"Relax, Red." Devon was shortening his life expectancy every time he called me that. "It'll take an hour, tops. Under the circumstances, you can spare an hour for your mother, can't you?"

If he was trying to lay the guilt trip on me, he was in for a rude awakening. "I can spare all the time in the world for my mother. In fact, I've already formed ideas about how to get those boxes back." I hadn't, but Devon didn't need to know that. In reality, Devon didn't need to be here. I was more than capable of finding our family's remains. I didn't need *Devon* for that. I didn't need *Devon* for anything.

"Can't wait to hear them. Bring them with you tomorrow."

I should have come up with a clever retort. I mean, I *could* have. I was more than skilled at clever retorts, but he was grinning at me, and I became increasingly aware his smile had a weird and dangerous effect on my equilibrium.

"Kate, I'm going to need a description of the boxes. What's in them, exactly what they looked like, and if they had any distinguishing marks. Babs, I'll need to know who came to your yard sale. I'm assuming you didn't draw a large crowd. Just the locals?"

It seemed Devon had successfully wrangled it so I had to work with him. Though why, I had no clue.

CHAPTER FOUR

I WAS NOT AT MY SOCIAL BEST FIRST THING IN THE MORNING. I COULD do early because, as an outdoor photographer, early was essential, but I typically flew solo at that hour. There was no need to be sociable or even dressed, for that matter. If I really wanted, I could haul it out to the trail in my PJs, but meeting Devon at the café meant at least looking presentable. I could understand him wanting to get an early start, but I couldn't understand why he needed my camera. The boxes were gone. With nothing to photograph, I had to wonder if Devon had a clue as to what he was doing.

I arrived first and found a small corner table at which to hide. I pulled my laptop out of my backpack and started working on my next post. I might as well get something accomplished while I waited. Engrossed with my work, I didn't notice anyone coming up behind me—not a good thing for a single girl living on her own, but then I suffered a familiar tug, and two things happened at once.

First, I remembered all those times Devon pulled on my hair. Only in those days, I wore pigtails. Since then, I'd graduated to a French braid. The second thing was lucky for Devon because I nearly tossed my coffee on him. I didn't, but only because the coffee was superb, and I didn't want to waste it.

"Morning, Red!"

It may have been worth losing the coffee after all.

"Sit, MacGyver, and let's get this over with." I pointed at the chair opposite me while trying not to grit my teeth.

"Yes, ma'am." He shook his head and laughed.

"Okay, Devon, what's so funny?"

"You, Pip. Still a spitfire, aren't you?" He set down his coffee, then sat and leaned back in his chair, which seemed to be his pattern. "So, have you ever looked in the boxes?" he asked without preamble.

I shook my head. "No. Ashes aren't my thing."

"How big were they?"

"The boxes? They're shoeboxes, Dev. Normal size."

He leaned in, and his cologne, like fresh rain, teased my senses.

"Don't you think maybe everyone is just a bit obsessed about this? I mean, they're ashes, not diamonds, right?"

"Maybe for my mom, they *are* diamonds. You'd feel different if they were your parents, wouldn't you?" That was a bit low, even for me, but he really couldn't be that dense.

"I see your point, but as you said, they're *your* relatives, and yet Matilda is just as determined to get them back. Same with Hope and Pru."

"You know how they are; all for one and one for all. Or is it the other way around?"

Devon frowned for a second. "If the boxes contained only ashes, why weren't they returned? Assuming whoever bought them opened them, why the hell haven't they brought them back?"

"You think I haven't thought of that?" I sighed because he had to think I was a complete idiot or didn't care. Unfortunately, the answer might simply be because whatever was in those boxes wasn't just ashes, but I hadn't figured out how to bring up the subject with my mother. She could have a quick temper, and I certainly didn't want to accuse her of anything.

He raised a brow. "You know what's in them, don't you?"

I didn't know whether he was being facetious or accusatory. It was hard to tell, so I didn't answer. I took a slow sip of my coffee and savored the moment. Silence, it seemed, was the perfect option.

"All right, let's get to your mom's. We'll take some photos."

"Of what? Empty shelves?"

"Exactly. We'll take my car."

I had no idea what he was driving, but I knew it had to be in better shape than mine. My Jeep had done its share of road trips, along with a few inadvertent off-road excursions, and it showed. On that basis, I agreed, even though he hadn't asked for my preference.

A few minutes later, we pulled up at my mother's house in his nondescript sedan, and while I may not have been at my social best early in the morning, my mother was. She answered the door, not in a robe, a housecoat, or even leggings. No, she was perfectly put together. Makeup? Check. Hair? Check. Perkiness? Check.

She gave me the once-over, then gave Devon a few air kisses. "Don't just stand there letting the moths in," she said, ushering us in.

"Not to worry, Kate, we'll be in and out before you know it. Pippa is just going to snap a few pictures, which may provide a few clues to get our investigation off the ground."

I glared at him because his assumptions were too much. I hadn't agreed to do any such thing! Taking pictures of empty shelves to provide clues seemed absurd, but the faster I got the job done, the sooner I'd be on my way. So, I immediately headed toward the infamous closet with Devon close behind.

When we reached the closet, I stopped short and turned—smack bang into his chest and rock-hard abs. Ignoring the desire to ensure those muscles were real, I cleared my throat. "What precisely do you need pictures of?"

"The shelves where the boxes were." He shrugged as if it were obvious. It wasn't obvious to me.

"Why?"

"Because the boxes have been there a long time. They'll leave an imprint." He pointed at the shelves, slightly tipping his head down while raising his brows as if to say, *go on... Do your job.*

Wanting to get the ordeal over with, I climbed the step stool then snapped away, getting as many shots as possible at different angles while batting his annoying pointing finger away.

"There and there," he said as if I couldn't see for myself.

"Devon, I have eyes. They are open. I am a photojournalist. Put. Your. Finger. Down."

That at least stopped the finger-pointing. It didn't stop the hovering though. Thankfully, there were only three shelves, which piqued my curiosity. While perched on the stool, I realized it would have been far easier for my mom to place the rug on the first shelf, not the top one, considering her height deficiency. If she had, perhaps we'd only be down one or two uncles instead of an entire branch of the family tree. Maybe my dad had put the rug on the shelf. Regardless, I still thought it best not to mention my involvement in taking down the boxes in the first place.

We returned to the front parlor, where my mother waited patiently. Devon asked her a few more questions about the boxes, and while I should have paid more attention, I was anxious to get on the trail. I had a few miles to hike, and it was essential to get to the meadow when the sun hit at just the right angle. Otherwise, the trip would be wasted.

No sooner were we back in the car when Devon smiled at me.

"What do you say, Red? Can I join you? Haven't been hiking in a while. Plus, I'd like to see what it is you do now."

"Bad idea, Dev. You'd be bored. Besides, you have a case to solve. How about you drop me at my Jeep, and you can go along on your merry way?"

He laughed. "Get over it, Red. I'm coming along."

His reply instantly reminded me that no matter how good-looking he might be, I still wanted to watch him walk across burning coals while a pack of hyenas chased him. The fact he wore hiking boots, jeans, and flannel layered over a t-shirt clearly meant he'd planned to go on my hike before he'd even got up that morning. Not going to happen if I could help it.

"Did you bring enough water? What about food? I'd share, but I only packed enough for one. Sorry." I smiled, trying to exude confidence, but I should have known he wouldn't give up that easily.

Devon also smiled, but his confidence was unfeigned. "Don't worry. I've got everything I need."

I didn't have another set of excuses, and I doubted Devon would simply accept my demand to leave me alone, which meant I now had a hiking buddy.

We picked up my Jeep, then headed to the foothills. Though spring was short-lived in the Rockies, the colorful wildflowers, rolling green meadows, and snow-capped peaks always took my breath away, especially with how the brilliant blue skies dotted with occasional puffs of white blanketed it all.

Surprisingly, Devon was well prepared for a hike. Considering he was a classic nerd, I'd assumed he'd gone to the mall and bought his gear the night before, but it was better than mine and obviously used. I was pretty sure he wasn't a private investigator and doubly convinced what he did for a living wasn't routine.

About a mile up the trailhead, I paused to get a few shots of the aspen trees, freshly painted with spring green leaves, and surrounded by beds of columbine in shades of blue and lilac.

"Tell me, Devon," I said, playing casual as I adjusted the lens on my camera. "What exactly is it that you do for a living?"

"Clearly, Red, I thought we established that. I investigate things."

"Clearly, Inspector Clouseau, that's not a good answer. Who do you investigate things for?"

"Depends. Right now, I'm investigating some missing shoeboxes for your mother." He grinned.

Well, that didn't tell me much. We hiked in silence for a bit. The variety of wildflowers changed from late spring through summer, but it was as if a rainbow suddenly pixelated in early spring, and all the little pieces fell to the ground. I took off for the center of the stunning field, in my element and totally absorbed—until Devon ended up in my line of sight. As he crouched and examined something, the light glistened off his mop of wavy, sun-kissed brown hair, which was how I ended with a few dozen photos of Devon Marks, PI, amidst a wild garden of color.

When he saw me snapping away, he held up his hand. "No pictures, Red. Sorry."

I frowned. "Come again?"

"You can't post any pictures of me online."

"Why? Are you in the witness protection program? Or a fugitive on the ten most wanted list?"

"No, and no. You'll just have to trust me on this one."

I wasn't sure where he got the idea I would trust him on

anything. Devon was still the boy who used to put rubber spiders inside my coat pocket. He'd have to do better than telling me to trust him. Arguing would have to wait, however, as I had flowers to capture and only a few hours of good light left.

A couple of hours later, we took a short break for lunch. I'd brought my usual nuts, cheese, and fruit. Devon munched on high protein power bars. I had to give him one thing; he didn't try and make small talk or annoy me any further. We just relaxed in the meadow, soaked up some spring sun, and enjoyed the vista. The day had really turned out to be perfect. Sneaking a glance at Devon, I wondered whether his soft smile meant he thought the same.

The ride back was uneventful, though an element of tension filled the Jeep. He fiddled with the radio until he landed on something country and twangy, but I changed it back to indie folk. His choice of music wasn't the reason for the tension—but I couldn't put my finger on what caused it.

Back at the café, I dropped him off at his car. He climbed out of my Jeep, and though I was sure he was about to say something, I gave him a short salute. "See ya."

I didn't wait for him to answer. Instead, I drove home as I had a bottle of wine I needed to open and a blog I needed to write.

CHAPTER FIVE

I STOPPED TO GET THE MAIL AT THE END OF MY DRIVEWAY AND FOUND A postcard from Las Vegas, Nevada, in the short stack of letters. The card was one of those tacky shots of the old Vegas sign—the landmark one with the red letters in the odd squishy diamond shape. I didn't know a soul in Vegas. I flipped the card over, and it had the oddest scribble.

We know you took it, so give it back, or you will pay. Dearly.

It didn't have my name on it, and I didn't see a stamp, meaning someone had stuck the postcard in my mailbox. I had absolutely no idea what the words were alluding to, but they were clearly a threat, and I couldn't control a shudder at the thought of heading into the house alone. Normally, my first reaction would be to call my best friend Dani, but she was deep-sea diving in Bali. So, I did the next best thing. I called my dad... He'd always been my go-to when I needed to feel safe.

"Dad?"

"Pippa? What's going on? What do you need?" He clearly recognized the slight worry in my voice.

"There's a nasty card in my mailbox. Someone thinks I took

something of theirs, and they want it back." Saying it out loud made it all sound a bit surreal.

"What does it say, exactly, sweetie?" His voice was calming and allowed me to relax, and I read it back to him.

"I'm sure it's a mistake, but why don't you bring it by the shop? Let me take a look."

"Okay, I'll be there in a few minutes," I said as I quickly headed back to my car.

Ye Olde Antique Shoppe, the family antique store where my dad pretty much spent most of his time, was right in the heart of downtown Luckland and was the perfect business for a fully restored frontier town. Luckland certainly had charm, at least enough to bring in the summer tourists, which benefitted sales. A magician when it came to restoration, my dad could transform anything from old and worn to profitable. Once he'd restored the items, I photographed them and posted them on our website, which I also managed.

My mom also worked in the shop, but her contribution to the business was online transactions, bookkeeping, and "air dusting"—which meant she would wander around the shop, gently blowing dust off the items. Her special talent was finding awesome antiques, but she tended to overbuy. There often wasn't enough room in the shop for everything, so she'd pick "just a few" items to bring home with her, which was how her house became so cluttered.

I pulled into the small parking lot to the rear of the shop, expecting to get a reassuring talk from my dad. Instead, I spotted Devon's rental car, and my blood pressure instantly rose. Yes, we'd been civil toward one another earlier, but fraught with nerves about the postcard, I didn't really want to have to deal with Devon twice in one day. He'd invaded my time and space enough already.

I bit back a curse and climbed out of my car while trying to figure out why Devon was there. It could be a coincidence, but I had a feeling Devon didn't do coincidental. Damn Devon and my reaction toward him. I wished I could simply ignore him, but that had never been the case—he'd always made sure of it. Frustrated, I crossed the parking lot, then stopped when the hairs at the back of my neck suddenly stood on end.

Turning slowly, I scoured the area but didn't see anything, yet I had an extraordinary feeling someone was watching me. A cold chill slid down my spine, pushing me to run the few feet to the shop's back door. As I pulled the door open, it set off the little bells that had hung there my entire life, and I didn't think I'd ever been so happy to hear them.

My dad, a big bear of a man who resembled a lumberjack with his fiery red hair and full beard, was the epitome of comfort. I gave him a hug as I always did, though I admit to holding him tighter than normal, then I took a seat on one of the elaborate throne chairs that had been in the store forever. Everyone admired the high-back, ornately carved Victorian chairs, yet nobody ever bought them. Personally, I hoped they never sold as I'd learned to climb up and sit on the chairs before I learned to walk. They also gave me a royal view of everyone's comings and goings, which was how I spotted Devon heading toward me with a half-smirk and a raised eyebrow.

My dad, of course, quickly apologized when he saw me glaring.

"Sorry, Punkin, but sometimes even I need reinforcements. You had me worried, so I figured Devon could help, being a PI, and all."

At least my dad understood my long-simmering animosity toward Devon. Most people would tell me to grow up, to let it go. It wasn't as if anything specifically horrid or tragic had occurred between Devon and me while growing up—it was simply that he was a total pain in the ass who managed to interfere with virtually everything I ever did. On my first movie date, the idiot sat three rows behind us and threw popcorn at us. The first time I sneaked out of the house, he ratted me out. The first time I wore a two-piece swimsuit, he laughed. So, if I harbored any resentment, it was clearly justified.

"Let me see the card." Devon held out his hand, covered in an evidence glove as if he were on an episode of CSI.

"Why are you wearing those things?" I asked as I grudgingly handed the postcard over.

He offered no response, which seemed to be his modus operandi. Though, in fairness, he was busy studying the card.

My dad picked up an old lamp and started cleaning it. I guess he thought everything would be fine now Devon had taken over. I supposed that was a good thing. Thankfully, my mom wasn't around. Either she would have reacted like an ice queen and told me I was being silly, or she would have called the FBI in a panic. There was no middle ground with her. Damn it, maybe I should have called Babs, but she wasn't much better. She'd probably convince me I had a stalker or something.

The feeling I had out in the parking lot returned, and I wondered if I should tell Devon about it. Probably not. I didn't want to start acting like a victim when the card turned out to be perfectly innocent. Most likely, someone had left the card at my house by accident, having gotten the wrong address. Regard-less, I wasn't ready to go home, though coffee and pie at the café sounded like a good idea. I doubted anything could happen to me in a public place, so I headed to the door.

"Hold up, Red."

I groaned. How could three little words get me so fired up?

"Where are you going?"

Though I didn't want to tell him, I had a feeling he'd find out anyway. "To the café. I'm in need of coffee." Not waiting for his reply or permission, I continued toward the exit.

Devon barreled right past me to open the door, then held it for me as if I were unable to execute such a simple action. Ignoring him, I headed to my Jeep, got in, slammed the door a tad too hard, and caught my bootlace in it. There was no graceful way to open the car door and untangle my shoelace, so I did it ungracefully, causing Devon to shake his head and snicker—which really was unnecessary.

"I heard that," I yelled out the window. I started up the Jeep and triumphantly peeled out of the parking lot. Unfortunately, Devon tailed close behind. By the time I'd driven to the café, which was less than a minute away, I realized he was following me. Fine. He could make sure no one lurked inside my house. So, I drove home.

Watching him surreptitiously as he checked out all the rooms made me feel a little better, but then he just stood in the middle of my kitchen until I realized he intended to stay. With a sigh, I gestured toward the fridge.

"I suppose you're hungry?"

"I could eat."

Considering I wasn't planning on company, I threw together some sandwiches and offered him a beer. At no point during our meal did Devon say anything—not about the postcard nor my doubtless irrational anxiety, which he'd obviously picked up on.

After he'd finished eating, he took his plate to the sink, grabbed another beer from the fridge, then made himself at home in my family room. Once again, as he'd done at my mom's house, Devon parked himself in the recliner.

"Maybe you could sit on the couch and let me have my recliner," I said in my best, super sweet voice.

"Nah, I'm good."

When he grabbed the remote and turned on a basketball game, I should have said something because apparently, allowing him to sit in the recliner was tacit approval to go full-on game night. Just when I was ready to blast him with both barrels, he turned to look at me and changed the subject.

"Ever been to Vegas, Red?"

The postcard. Good. Hopefully, I'd get his opinion on it. "No." I waited for him to ask the next question, but after a moment, he shrugged. I frowned at his lack of concern, but if he wasn't worried about it, maybe I shouldn't be either. Maybe he thought the same thing I did, that it was delivered to me by accident.

"I called Aunt Tillie on the way over to let her know I'll be staying a few days."

My frown deepened. "Didn't she already know?" She had to have known, and why was Devon changing subjects again? To put me off balance?

"I meant here. At your place," Devon said.

I was sure the look I gave him was similar to a bunny caught in the middle of a road, dazed by headlights. Devon Marks, the excruciatingly annoying, intensely good-looking bane of my existence, thought he was staying at my place for a few days? No way.

"Why would you want to stay here if you're not worried about the postcard?"

"I never said that."

"You—" So he was worried? I ignored the shiver that raced down my spine. "What if I don't have room? What if I'm expecting company?"

"You do, and you're not."

Now while that may have been true, how did he know? It must have been Matilda. She'd most likely told him every tiny detail of my life. Matilda at her finest was a perfect conniver. I just didn't know what she was up to this time. I had my suspicions, of course, but I would need some verification, and I knew just where to get it.

"I'm just gonna make a quick call." I figured he'd be so focused on the game he wouldn't even acknowledge I'd said anything. However, he looked over and winked.

"You go right ahead, Pip. It won't make a difference."

"I don't know what you mean," I muttered, grabbing my phone as I headed out to the back porch and over to the little concrete bench I'd placed out by the garden. Thanks to the help of some of the employees at the local nursery, I actually had a garden. I gave them free publicity on the blog; they gave me seeds and advice, and it worked out splendidly.

It irritated me that Devon seemed to think he knew what I was going to do before I even did it, but it irritated me more that he was right. I had planned to call Matilda to get him out of my hair. Instead, I called Prudence, who by that time would be primed and ready to talk. Generally loose-lipped most of the time, it was far easier to get her to spill the beans by mid-evening.

The ringtone went on forever, and I was just about ready to hang up when Prudence finally answered.

"Pip, dear, what's up?" She sounded out of breath.

"Did you hear about the postcard?" I asked, starting off with something simple to test the waters.

"What card is that?"

"Never mind, just tell me one thing. Is Matilda up to something? Is she trying to, I don't know, set me up?"

"Whyever would she do that? I mean, yes, we all think it's about time you found someone, but right now, we need to focus on the boxes. Though, you know, with Devon back in town, it wouldn't hurt for you to—"

"Gotta run, Pru, thanks!" I disconnected and frowned. It seemed I was right. Matilda was matchmaking. Maybe she planted the card in the mailbox...

I tried to sneak back into my house after my little chat with Prudence, which, rather than producing anything fruitful, simply served to make me even more nervous. I wasn't ready to deal with Devon in my home, especially since I'd started to notice the little smiles he threw my way and how they turned my stomach into a tight little knot. Considering our past, I had no idea where this new and inexplicable attraction came from, but there was no way I could deny it. I also couldn't deny feeling a whole lot safer with him here after getting that post-card. Despite thinking the card might not have anything to do with me, someone out there thought the occupant of this house had something they wanted back, so having Devon around was preferable to being alone if anyone tried to crawl in the back window. I sighed, then figured I would get the guest room fixed up and toss a pillow at him. That should be enough for one night.

"Have a nice chat with Pru?"

"What, are you eavesdropping now?" That was too much. How could he have known I'd called Prudence? In fact, I didn't understand why I'd bothered calling anyone—I should have asked Devon outright.

"Okay, Agent Mulder. Spill it. You seem to know way more than I do about what's going on around here. My version? Babs accidentally sold a bunch of ashes. Your version? Not even close. So. Clue me in. What are you doing here? And don't BS me."

"Are you always this dramatic? Just sit down, would you?"

That was Devon at his most annoying. I sat, but for no other reason than wanting info. "Okay, I'm sitting. Now, how did you know I was talking to Prudence? That's my first question."

"I called Aunt Tillie to let her know you'd agreed to me

staying here. She said Hope was calling then she put me on hold. She came back on and said Hope had been talking to Prudence when you called her."

I found that all a bit convoluted, but I nodded. "Next question, what are you doing back in Luckland? Are you really here to find the boxes? Or did Matilda have some other reason for bringing you?"

"That's three questions. Look, why don't you show me those photos you took?"

Frustrated at his stonewalling, I complied, but only because if I didn't, I'd end up punching him or something. Not that I condoned violence, but the man was *seriously* infuriating. I got my laptop and pulled up the photo file for that day's shoot. I thought they were stunning—even the ones without Devon in them.

Devon shook his head. "No. The shelves? Remember?"

"Silly me, I don't know how I could have forgotten such a visually stimulating set of shots." By his smirk, my sarcasm wasn't lost on him. I opened the other folder, the one I'd labeled "empty shelves," then handed him the laptop, worried I might hit him over the head with it. Before I did something violent, I stood and headed toward the stairs. "Have at it."

As soon as I reached the top of the stairs, I realized what I'd done. I had left him alone with my laptop. My entire life was on there. I considered running back down and yanking it away, but if I did, Devon would know I was trying to hide something from him. I just hoped he'd look at the photos of the shelves and not go searching through the rest of my stuff.

Trying not to think about it, I went into the guest room and made sure the linens weren't too dusty before taking out a little aggression on the pillow. Then I grabbed some clean towels and neatly placed them on the dresser—without even for a nanosecond, imagining Devon in nothing but a towel. When I headed back downstairs, he intently stared at the screen and scribbled on a notepad. A notepad? I walked over and peered over his shoulder. He was just writing down numbers—notations that reminded me of math class.

"What are you doing?" I asked, which was a perfectly legit question.

"Measurements."

"Right. Listen, Columbo, they were shoeboxes. I have lots of them upstairs. Can't you just measure one?" Another perfectly legit question.

"You know not all boxes are alike. Even shoeboxes. Different facilities manufacture their boxes with subtle variations. Also, measurements change over time, so you can easily see why it's important to know the size of each box. Then we can start tracing."

"You're going to trace shoeboxes?"

"But of course. That way, we'll know what we're looking for."

"All that aside, you do realize each box is labeled. You'd know them if you saw them," I said as nicely as I could.

"Listen, Red. You stick to your photography and let me do the investigating. I don't suppose you have any cookies, do you?"

"All out. Your room is upstairs on the left," I replied, perhaps a bit sharply. Then I smacked his hand from my laptop and yanked it from him before I headed back upstairs. Even though I had an unopened box of cookies from the bakery, I certainly wasn't about to share after his derogatory comments.

CHAPTER SIX

Coffee was a necessity for me. It was my morning nirvana. I simply didn't function at full capacity until I'd consumed at least one generous mug full, which was why, when I entered the kitchen early the following morning and found Devon in the middle of it, I froze for just a moment, then spun right around and headed back upstairs. I didn't want Devon, of all people, to see me in my PJs and sports bra, and my annoyance only abated when the savory aroma of bacon wafted through the house. I was sure I didn't have any bacon. Then again, I hadn't cleaned out the freezer in a week, or maybe a month, maybe two. I wondered if he had found the eggs as well. Perhaps if I waited a few minutes, I'd arrive downstairs to breakfast, which would actually be an excellent start to the day.

I threw on a t-shirt then ran a comb through my hair. I admit I did a little tweaking because there was no need to look like the bride of Frankenstein's monster, then headed back down to find the kitchen table fully laden with food. There were scrambled eggs, bacon, toasted English muffins, and even a cup of coffee waiting. However, the sight of Devon standing there like a TV chef threw me for a loop. I wasn't sure why he'd gone and prepared such a feast, and quite frankly, I didn't particularly care. I sat and smiled at my new personal chef, picked up a fork, and dove in.

"Wow. I mean, this is delicious," I said around a mouthful.

"Glad you like it." He looked at me curiously. "Were you out of town recently?"

"No, why?"

"Hmm. The pantry is a bit...sparse. I couldn't find anything to season with."

"Well, you know how it is. I don't get to cook much." I quickly began to focus back on the food as there was no need to bring up my lack of cooking skills or any actual desire to cook, even though my little rental happened to have a true chef's kitchen with a fabulous gas cooktop on a quartz island.

"Did I mention Aunt Tillie wants us all to come for dinner tonight?" Devon asked, his tone casual. I *had* hoped he would change the subject, but this was comparable to dropping a bomb.

"You did not. I'm not sure I'm up for it." Matilda's dinners were infamous. Not just for the attendees, but for the thematic and often dramatic approach she always took.

"Because of the postcard? You'll be perfectly safe at Matilda's. You know that. Anyway, I'll be with you." Devon looked at me so sincerely I bit back anything snarky. Instead, I decided it was time for some honesty.

"Yesterday, when I came to the shop to show Dad the card, I thought—no—I felt as if someone were watching me."

Devon frowned. "You should have told me. Did you see anyone?" His tone was calm, but his eyes held a sharp alertness.

"No. It was just a sense, you know? I guess I *was* spooked because of the postcard, which was silly considering whoever dropped it off probably got the wrong house." I added that last bit to get Devon's reaction. I really wanted him to agree with me.

The expression on his face softened. "Even so, maybe being with everyone tonight will settle your nerves. Also, we don't have to be there until five, which leaves plenty of time for us to go shoebox hunting."

"Shoebox hunting? You told me to let *you* do the investigating. Anyway, in case you hadn't noticed, I'm not the box-hunting type."

"Because you have never gone box-hunting with me. Trust me. You'll love it." He gave me that melting wink and a grin, which had begun to act like some sort of on-and-off switch for my hormones, then he sauntered back upstairs, leaving every dish and pan for me to clean up. I sighed. Just as I'd started to think he might have had some redeeming qualities, he ruined it.

As soon as I'd cleaned the kitchen, Devon returned and clued me in on his itinerary.

"Here's what I'm thinking, Pip. We'll head to the shop first as I have some questions for your mom. I want to take a look around town as well," he said in that charming way of his, which meant he didn't ask me or give me a chance to offer my opinion. I almost wanted to argue, but I'd planned to go to the shop sometime that day anyway.

"Fine by me. I'll bring my laptop and get a little work done."

All the way to the shop, I threw little glances at Devon. He wore well-worn jeans, his hiking boots, and a plain black t-shirt that really seemed a little small for his broad shoulders, though it showed off his flat stomach to perfection. At a set of traffic lights, he turned to see me checking out his muscular thighs, and despite pretending I was glancing out the window, I caught his grin. The man missed nothing, and I needed to remember that.

When we arrived at the shop, I headed to the throne chairs,

but the chairs were gone. For a second, I stood and stared at the spot they'd always stood, then I scoured the store, wondering if my mom or dad had moved them, but when I couldn't find them anywhere, I made a beeline to the front of the store where my dad was showing Devon a warlord's mask my dad had found on eBay.

"Dad. The chairs? Where are they?" In total panic mode, I interrupted them without a second thought.

"Oh, Pippa, you won't believe this. We had a banner morning. Sold those chairs, the twelve-foot table, even that highboy. New people bought the Tindle place. Funny thing, I didn't even know it was for sale."

My mother stopped her "air dusting" and joined the conversation. "Seems the new owners, two very nice gentlemen, just moved back from Seychelles and left all their furniture behind. Isn't it wonderful?"

Wonderful? No, it wasn't wonderful. My life was now the *opposite* of wonderful. First the boxes, then the threatening postcard, now eccentric wealthy new neighbors had run off with my throne chairs. It was as if the universe were messing with me.

"Yeah, wonderful." I couldn't help that my tone was flat, and it seemed Devon picked up on my mood.

"Pip, how about we head off."

"Where are we going?"

"Yard sale."

I should have known. Saturday was yard sale day in Luckland, but I'd had enough of yard sales. I could have told him to go alone, but I doubted that would go over well. After saying goodbye to my parents, I followed Devon out to his car.

As we pulled up to the first house, I turned to him. "You think whoever bought the boxes is reselling them at their own yard sale, don't you? Like regifting?" I allowed a slightly sarcastic hint to my voice. He smiled at my attempted humor but didn't say anything. Instead, he came around to open my door. Having someone open a door for me was a little disconcerting. My first instinct was to scoff but appreciating his efforts might work in my favor.

"Thanks."

His smile turned a tad brighter. "Why don't you look around and see who's here."

I wasn't sure what the point was as I had no idea who turned up to Babs's yard sale, but I was an avid people watcher, so I nodded.

Most browsers who milled about looking for treasure while surreptitiously checking the prices were known entities. Lois Thorpe and her sister Louise, Mrs. Jenkins, my old high school math teacher, who chased after her grandkids, and Tommy Thistle, the local mechanic, on his weekly hunt for scrap parts. As I looked around, it seemed half the neighborhood had turned up. Then I spotted two men I'd not seen before... They were older, perhaps closer to my dad's age, and they seemed just a tad eccentric, at least from their attire. They each wore off-the-rack western outfits, and by western, I meant button-down shirts tucked into brand-new jeans with large, somewhat tacky belt buckles, cowboy boots, and...cowboy hats. Luckland *was* an old frontier town, so it wasn't totally unheard of for people to think they should be wearing "western" attire. I nudged Devon.

"You think those are the guys who bought the Tindle house and the furniture?"

He didn't look at me as he seemed to be watching them too. "I'd say it's likely. Maybe you could take a few pics?"

"Of them?"

"Yeah, but don't make it obvious."

I grinned then meandered through the maze of tables

covered with knickknacks, old lava lamps, and mismatched Tupperware. Nobody paid any attention to my camera or me as they were all accustomed to my photo frenzies. By the time Devon was ready to leave, he'd evidently bought himself several items he'd tucked neatly away in a brown sack.

"Whatcha got there, Curious George?" What he could have possibly purchased was beyond me. I couldn't recall the last time I found a single guy at a local yard sale picking up knickknacks.

"I suppose that's for me to know and you to find out. Perhaps." He gave me that wicked grin again—the one that flipped my stomach upside down.

"It's not a surprise for me, is it? Because I needn't remind you, I'm not fond of surprises, especially where you're concerned."

His grin widened, and I decided now wasn't the moment to start dredging up old memories. We had at least three more yard sales to get to and only so many hours to do it in. I was exhausted by the time we were through, and we barely made it back home to change and get over to Matilda's, a stickler for people arriving on time.

At that point, Devon and I seemed to have called a truce, mainly because he hadn't uttered the term "Red" all day. I wasn't naive. It was coming, and when I least expected it, so I had to be ready at all times.

That evening's festivities were typical of Matilda. She'd invited everyone. Prudence. My folks. Babs and Tom. Hope and her fiancée, Marcy. Everyone was out on the deck, enjoying a cocktail and Hope's famous appetizer platter. For years we'd all relied on Hope and Marcy for fabulous food. They were astonishingly talented in the kitchen, and the couple owned the Blue Sky Café, where Devon and I had met for coffee. After realizing the hours were practically twenty-four seven, they hired a staff of cooks and servers to handle the day-to-day activities. Hope and Marcy still controlled the menu and the overall operations, but neither enjoyed getting up early nor working late.

Matilda's soirée featured a caprese salad with homemade mozzarella, fresh basil, and freshly baked rustic garlic bread. The aroma was heavenly—the theme evidently Italian.

I poured myself a glass of wine, grabbed a plate of food, then headed off to my favorite comfy cushioned chair in the corner. Everyone knew I always sat there, including Devon, but he got there first. It was one of those long chaise lounge chairs, so there was plenty of room for two, but he'd spread out, taking all of it.

"Devon, as comfortable as you look right now, you don't need to take up the whole seat. Move your legs and let me sit, and don't even think of refusing."

He glanced up at me, grinned, then swung his legs over the side. I momentarily relaxed but sitting that close reinforced how different grown-up Devon was from his teenage self. I became aware of his cologne—a spicy mix of woodsy and citrus. I also became aware of the heat from his body, now just inches from mine. If I moved slightly to the left, I could have brushed his shoulder with mine, or rested my head on his chest, or...

Everybody gave us knowing glances that seemed to say they thought they knew a secret. They couldn't have been more wrong. I hated being the center of gossip, so to prevent wagging tongues, I scrambled off the chair and headed to the rail twenty feet away on the opposite side of the deck.

"What's up with you and Devon?" Babs asked, going straight for the jugular.

"Not a darn thing, Babs. Leave it alone."

At that point, Tom sauntered up, looking as if he was on his second or possibly third drink.

"What's up with you and Devon?" he asked. His eyes gleamed as he gestured with a nod and a lift of his glass.

"Nada. Zilch. Zippo is *up* with Devon and me."

"Well, that's not what Pru said," he replied with a smirk.

"Is nothing sacred around here?" I sighed in defeat. I'd given up the comfy chair to avoid the inquisition and got one anyway.

Just then, Matilda called everyone inside to take their seats for dinner. As usual, Hope and Marcy brought the food. I'd started to wonder if Matilda, like me, hardly ever cooked. Devon's breakfast skills were pretty damn good, so I assumed he'd learned to cook for himself. I made a mental note to ask him.

The dining table was super long, seating all of us comfortably with name cards at every place.

"Devon, what have you learned? Where are the boxes?" Matilda asked, holding court once everyone had found their seat.

"Aunt Tillie, you know I haven't found them yet. From what I can tell, it's just a misunderstanding, and whoever has them probably hasn't even opened them. In fact, Pippa took some pictures today at the yard sales, and we can all take a look after dinner. It might inspire us."

There was a murmur of assent around the table and what oddly felt like an air of excitement. I just wasn't sure why. Plus, I hadn't brought my laptop or my camera, so I wasn't sure how I could show them anything. If Devon had wanted me to bring either one, he really should have told me. It seemed he and I needed to work on our communication skills.

My mom cleared her throat and waited for everyone to hush up. "My news is quite fascinating. Colin and I have met the newest residents in Luckland! A lovely old pair from an exotic island in the Indian Ocean. They came into the shop and practically furnished their entire place. They bought the Tindle estate, you know."

As we didn't get new residents in Luckland often, this was a hot topic. So, with the shoeboxes now forgotten, it seemed we were on to town gossip.

"I heard they were treasure hunters who'd just returned from a deep-sea dive to a sunken pirate ship," my dad said.

"Well, I heard they paid upward of half a million for the Tindle place," Marcy said. "*In cash.*"

"I wonder if it really is haunted," Hope said. "Maybe they'll invite us in. Then we can finally see what's hiding behind those old walls!"

"I ran into them at the Super Saver, over in the baking section," Prudence said. "Utterly charming. I was sure the tall one was going to ask me out until Lois Thorpe came over and batted her fake eyelashes."

While their anecdotes were amusing, I had a hunch—an idea I couldn't quite shake as to why the two oddball men were in Luckland. So, I decided to toss it out there to see what everyone thought. "I think they are here for the gold." It surprised me that nobody else had thought of that. They all stared at me expectantly, so I expanded on my theory. "Everyone knows about the legend—that our town's founders followed a map to find gold. Because of that, each year, we cele-brate Founders' Day with a treasure hunt to attract tourists using 'lost gold' maps. Maybe the newest residents believe the gold is real."

Devon chuckled. "Nobody believes it's real."

"A lot of people believe the gold is real," Matilda said. "Our forefathers certainly did."

I internally winced. I should have realized mentioning the town's founders meant getting a history lesson.

"You know Pru, Kate, Hope, and I are all descended from the four Irish immigrants who founded this town in 1851."

Devon barely kept back a sigh. "Yes, I know that. I'm not dissing your ancestors—"

"They're your ancestors too, Devon," Matilda said, her tone a little sharp.

"Sorry," Devon said. "I merely wanted to state that even though they crossed the country to find gold, none was ever found. Or at least none we know of."

I clucked my tongue at his naivety. "I don't think that matters to the tourists or the town. Luckland's success is derived directly from the legend. Those copies of the map are for sale in every business in Luckland. Not to mention that Selby's Mercantile keeps panning supplies in stock year-round and sells little bags of fool's gold. To this day, nobody has ever seen a speck of real gold, but they keep trying. So, I honestly think those two men could very well be here to find it."

"Unless they're here because of our other legend," my mom said. "It's well known our ancestors built Luckland on sacred Native American ground, and our Founders' Day ritual keeps the spirits of those buried beneath and around the town appeased. If we don't do our ritual, the spirits of the dead will rise."

An uneasy look passed between the women, which seemed to have caught Devon's attention because he frowned.

"You think they're ghost hunters?" I asked, remembering stories of discontented ghouls frequenting our little town. Not that I'd ever seen any, but as far as I knew, talk of ghosts had been around for as long as the talk of gold.

"And everyone knows the Inn is haunted," Pru said.

The Inn was the only hotel in Luckland, and it accommo-dated the annual drove of tourists who came to find gold. I shook my head. It was far more feasible the men were here because of the gold, not ghosts, but then again, they certainly looked like an odd pair, so who knew.

I glanced at Devon to see if I could gauge his thoughts. He had that same expression he used to have in chemistry class during lab. Usually, a mild explosion of some sort usually followed that expression.

Dessert arrived, which was another stellar temptation in the way of a divinely dense cheesecake with fresh blackberry sauce. My sweet tooth was in fine form that night. Sadly, I was only two bites in when Babs crashed my moment.

"Can we talk about Pippa's stalker now?"

I shot her a look. "Stalker?" I'd only mentioned the feeling that someone was watching me to Devon. I narrowed my eyes at him, but he only seemed interested in dessert.

"Yeah, the postcard."

Oh, of course. Dad must have told her. In fact, everyone probably knew about the postcard by now, and though I'd initially assumed the feeling of being watched and the post-card were related, now I wasn't so sure. "No stalker, Babs. I'm sure the postcard was a misunderstanding. Just a wrong address."

I really didn't want the posse involved, nor did I care to have my life meddled with—and those women were the queens of meddling.

"Actually," Devon said. "It's definitely a concern."

I glared at him.

He glared right back. "Easy, Red." There it was. Truce over.

"Look, I'm not sure of anything yet. Maybe it was the wrong address, but I need to investigate thoroughly, and I promise you, I'll get to the bottom of it."

I bristled. "You mean *we'll* get to the bottom of it, don't you?"

He bit back a smile while shaking his head. "*We'll* get to the bottom of it. Why don't we start by reconvening in the living room?"

Reconvene. There was that word again. I didn't have much choice, but I did insist on finishing my cheesecake. Some things just took priority.

Once we'd all found a seat and settled in, except Devon, who remained standing, he began asking questions.

"Who in here has met the new neighbors? Just raise a hand."

I looked around. It seemed only my parents and Prudence had seen them.

"Who in here has heard a rumor or two about them?" Devon asked.

I thought that an odd question, but everyone raised their hand. Devon approached Babs and pulled out his phone, showing her the screen.

"Recognize them?" he asked.

I leaned over and craned my neck to see what he was showing her. The photo was from the yard sale of the two old cowboy wannabes. Devon was also in the shot—which meant I'd taken it, and he'd accessed my photo folder on my laptop. That man seemed to believe boundaries didn't exist, and I had to stop myself from gritting my teeth.

"Oh, why yes," Babs replied. "They were at my yard sale!"

"Do you remember what they bought?" Devon asked.

"No. Most everyone just put the money in the jar and took their things."

Devon nodded. "I see." He strode over to my dad and showed him the photo.

"Those were the two gentlemen in the store," my dad said, peering at the photo and nodding.

After going around the room, basically interviewing every-one, Devon slid his phone back into his pocket and leaned against the fireplace mantel. That was it. No conclusions, no "Hey, thanks," or "Sorry, Pippa, for snooping through your files." All Devon's "investigation" had determined was Luckland's newest residents liked yard sales and antiques, and none of that seemed relevant to the Vegas postcard. Unless his questions related to the missing shoeboxes, which, granted, was the reason he was here in Luckland.

"Well, now," Matilda said in her most cheerful voice. "Who's up for some karaoke?"

I almost groaned. Matilda McDonald was the Karaoke Queen of Luckland, and every *soirée* ended with a rousing round of Name That Tune. Granted, she did have quite the voice.

Devon and I didn't stay. I don't think either of us was in the mood. We drove back to my house in silence, and if his white-knuckled grip on the steering wheel was any indication, he seemed contemplative and tense. We pulled into the driveway, and I wondered if his anxiety was related to the postcard or the shoeboxes. Or something else. Neither of us said a word as we climbed the steps to the porch, but when I opened the front door, I froze and finally broke the awkward silence.

"What the bloody hell!"

CHAPTER SEVEN

My living room looked like the aftermath of a barroom brawl. Devon barreled right on in, blowing past me, and putting his arm out to stop me from entering.

"Call emergency services," he whispered. "And wait outside. Do it now."

His take-charge authoritarian manner should have irritated me, but there was no way I was going inside. I called for help and sat on the porch swing to wait while peeking through the window. The moonless night put the house's interior in shadows, with just a sliver of light acting like a beacon from the upstairs hall. Devon had his right arm extended in front of him, and I just knew he had a gun. I didn't see it, but I *had* seen enough movies and TV shows to recognize the silhouette. Fear, once more, sent chills down my spine as I recalled that moment in the parking lot where I'd thought someone had watched me.

I turned my attention to the street, checking every shadow, every movement until I almost thought I'd be safer inside the house than out. Devon was taking a long time in there, and I was on the verge of following him regardless of the danger that might lurk inside when one of the deputies arrived.

Luckland didn't have a local police department as it was too small a town for that, but the county sheriff had an office, so we were reasonably well-protected. At least, I thought we were.

Devon came out of the house and introduced himself to the female deputy, then spoke quietly for a minute, which was about as long as I was willing to remain sitting on the sidelines. I approached the two of them.

"Ms. O'Leary. This is your house, I believe," the deputy said. "Can you tell me what happened?"

"Well, there isn't much to tell. I started to unlock the door, only it was already unlocked, and when I opened it, I couldn't help but notice my house was trashed. I yelled something a bit colorful, then Devon went inside and told me to wait out here. Maybe Devon could share what he saw?"

The two exchanged looks, which oddly seemed ominous.

"Tell you what," the deputy said. "Let me go in and look around, and we'll talk more after that. Okay?"

I gave them each a look that told them I didn't exactly like having to comply, but I didn't have a choice, so I gave the deputy a brief but reluctant nod.

Devon went right in there with her, leaving me alone outside once again. I instantly went back on high alert. Whoever trashed my house could be hiding in the bushes. Checking out the shadows once more, I realized I was a sitting duck. What if someone kidnapped me? What if I ended up chopped into pieces and stuffed in an old, abandoned shed? My face could be on the cover of a milk carton and taped to telephone poles, or I could...

Two additional patrol cars pulled up. One was the sheriff's; I'd recognize the big SUV anywhere. The timing couldn't have been any better because it stopped my mind from going further down that dark, detrimental road.

Devon came back out just then and crouched next to me.

"Where's your laptop, Pip?" he asked gently. I took a breath and thought about where I had my laptop last.

"Try the kitchen table. Or maybe the coffee table. Wait, no, it could be upstairs?" My brain was not functioning well. He nodded then disappeared back into the house. My laptop? At that point, I realized it was probably gone. My life was now in the hands of thieves. Whether that was worse than being in Devon's hands, I wasn't sure. Thankfully, I'd backed up all the information in the cloud.

It felt as if an eternity had passed as I sat and watched the scene unfold. Officers traipsed in and out the front door and used crime scene tape. We didn't have a lot of crime in Luckland. It was probably the first time they'd had to use that stuff. It seemed to me they were taking things awfully seriously. The burning question was why they'd allowed Devon in the house, not me. I was quite sure private investigators didn't have special police privileges, which meant he wasn't a private investigator, though that left the question of what he was.

Eventually, they all packed up their gear, and Devon came and sat next to me on the porch swing.

"You okay, Red?"

I couldn't even find the strength to be annoyed at him calling me Red. In fact, there was something about his tone. It was oddly comforting—and maybe a little...sexy. Okay, maybe a lot. How my mind went in that direction after someone ransacked my home, I had no clue.

"Not really," I replied. "My camera?" He shook his head. That was my biggest nightmare. It was insured, but a good camera wasn't just a piece of equipment to me—it was an extension of who I was. That particular camera had been with me through some of my most excellent adventures.

Devon must have sensed my mood because he held out his hand to help me to my feet.

"Let's go," he said. "I'm dropping you at your mom's."

"Sorry, no dice. I haven't slept at my mom's in forever, Devon."

"Okay, I get it. Your dad's?"

"No! Seriously, Dev. She'll find out, and I'll never hear the end of it. Even though they live separately, they tell each other everything." I sighed. "Drop me at the Inn, okay?" At this time of year, the Inn would have rooms available.

"You'd rather go to the Inn than your mom's house? You might need to explain that one."

"I just know if I go to either parental's house, I'm going to be stuck having to have that conversation about living alone and blah blah blah. I know Matilda probably never does that to you since you're a guy, but my parents feel I could still live at home since I'm single. A bit archaic, I know.

"Maybe they just want your company. Maybe they like having you around."

I tipped my head and looked at him for signs of sarcasm, but there were none.

"Maybe, Devon. For now, let's stick with the Inn."

"Okay, Luckland Inn, it is." He seemed to accept it was my call, which made me feel a little more in control. I grabbed my overnight emergency bag with clean clothes and toiletries from the back of my Jeep. The hazards of being an outdoor photographer were many, and I always needed to be prepared.

However, when we reached the Inn in Devon's rental car, preparation and control seemed to go out the window as the sweet girl at the Inn's reception desk said they were full.

"I'm so very sorry. We had a sudden surge of tourists. It's too early for Founders' Day, so we can't figure it out. Jessa Sands said she thinks they wrote us up in the Denver Post. We do have one suite, but I'm not really supposed to rent it. It's not quite done."

I listened to her chatter away, but I could feel my cool shattering. No rooms. Except one. "I'll take it."

"Um, yes, but it hasn't been remodeled yet..."

"It's fine. I'll take it."

I turned to Devon. "Go ahead. You can go back to Matilda's. I'm perfectly safe here."

"Not happening, Red. Where you go, I go." He said that last bit quite seriously. "Of course, you can always come with me."

I contemplated it. There would be questions, and Matilda would alert the posse. So, no. Going to Matilda's would not be a prudent choice. However, if I stayed at the Inn, I'd be in a hotel room, with Devon. Only in the impossible life of Pippa O'Leary could that ever happen. Ultimately, exhaustion won out, and I chose what I thought would be the lesser of two evils.

As we headed up the ancient staircase, I thought I should prepare him.

"Devon, have you ever stayed here before? You know this place is old, right? As in ancient."

"Haven't stayed here, but I do know a bit about the place. You sure *you're* up for it?"

"Of course. You think I can't handle the fact it started out as a brothel?"

He grinned. "Oh, I've no doubt you can handle that part, but you do remember it's supposed to be haunted? Isn't the Scarlet Lady a famous sighting?"

I would have preferred seeing her to what I saw when I opened the door. I stopped in my tracks, put my bag down, and let out a huge breath. Blood-red satin sheets were on the bed, lace doilies on the dresser, and a fake bear rug on the floor. Someone must have decided to have some of the rooms looking as they would have done all those years ago. Thank god they were doing a makeover, but for now, I didn't think I could handle having such a reminder that sex was the order of the day back then, at least not with Devon in the room with me.

I turned to him. "Don't laugh."

"I wouldn't think of it."

I sat on what had to be the tackiest bed ever and spotted a velvet painting of dogs smoking cigars and playing poker. I looked up at Devon, who clearly struggled not to burst out laughing.

"Come on, Red. Let's hit the bar downstairs. I think we could use some downtime."

I was kind of getting used to the "Red" thing. At least it wasn't making my blood boil anymore.

Downstairs was no better regarding décor. There was, however, a bar, or rather, a saloon, and where there was a bar, I could usually find a bright side. Devon fetched us each a beer then we grabbed one of the few empty tables. I noticed Devon made sure to pick the seat facing the entrance. I read somewhere it was always safer to face the door. After thinking about that for a minute or two, I figured I would let him finish his beer, then see if I could get a little intel. Not that I was particularly good at probing and prodding for answer

The music was a little too loud and a little too country for me, and the noise from all the damn tourists sounded like a beehive. Devon, however, appeared relaxed, so I kept my opinions to myself. Like the suite upstairs, I noticed there was no TV in the bar. I wondered if this was a TV-free hotel. I'd never heard of that, but then again, maybe I hadn't stayed in enough ex-brothels to know. It meant we'd have to entertain ourselves, which could potentially require some sort of conversation—and not the monosyllabic kind.

To my surprise, Devon must have realized the same thing because he leaned forward, then crooked his finger at me in a "come closer" kind of fashion. Warily, I leaned in. I wouldn't have put it past him if he'd tugged on my hair or something, but he placed his lips close to my ear. His warm breath on my skin tickled and sent a flash of heat racing through my limbs. I quickly pulled back, and our gazes locked. I'd known Devon my entire life, yet just then, something...changed in my perception of him. Not the fact I'd already noticed how stunningly handsome he'd become, but something deeper, something a lot less definable. If someone had asked me to explain it, I would have said something shifted inside me. It was a strange sensation, and I wasn't particularly sure I liked it. I swallowed hard and hoped Devon didn't notice.

"These relatives of yours, the ones in the shoeboxes, did you ever meet any of them?" He spoke loud enough to make sure those around us couldn't hear him but for me to understand. How could I not? He was only inches away. So close I could feel his body temperature.

"Not a one. Why?"

"You must have seen pictures. Maybe a family photo album?"

I shook my head. "What are you thinking, Devon? Out with it." Being direct was the most effective measure with him. He'd never taken hints very well. He looked at me for a moment, studying me. Then as if he'd made a decision, he stood and grabbed my hand to pull me up.

"Let's go up to the room. We can't talk down here."

I nodded but tugged my hand from his, wondering if he also felt the zing that sent my heart racing.

Once we were back in the scarlet room, as I'd dubbed it, I took a seat with several calming breaths and waited for him to continue his train of thought.

"I find it odd you never saw any photos. Or met them. And before you say anything, just listen. My aunt loves your mom to pieces, but this whole thing seems quite personal for her. And the others. It's as if they share the same odd anxiety over the fact the shoeboxes have gone missing. It makes me wonder what we've missed." He paused and waited while I thought about it. He had a point.

"Well, you know you can always ask to see photos of the aunts and uncles. See what happens." I didn't have anything else to add because I couldn't really think past what had happened over the last few days. First, "losing" the boxes, then the note on the postcard, the feeling of someone watching me, someone breaking into my home, and lastly, having to deal with Devon twenty-four seven. Everything was emotionally draining. Well, not Devon exactly, more my conflicted feelings about him. He must have sensed my exhaustion because he nodded.

"Tell me about your blog. Is it just about flowers?"

I frowned, not really believing he wanted to know more about my blog. Very few people outside environmental groups, their followers, and the local botany association, cared one whit about my blog. Maybe his interest was a ploy to get me to forget about the break-in. He sounded sincere, though, and I gave him brownie points for effort.

"It's about all things outdoors. Whatever I can capture on my camera and share with readers. My blog is for those who've never been traveling outside their little corner of the world, so I bring it to them. It's interesting, and I love it. I want to do more." When he smiled, I realized this was my chance to ask him some questions about his job. "What about you? Do you enjoy what you do?"

He looked at me as if deciding what to tell me. Then he smiled.

"I've always loved solving puzzles. You know that. I love a good mystery and figuring out the clues. I guess if I have to work for a living, at least I can have some fun."

I wanted to ask him about the gun, but I didn't think now was the right time, so I changed gears.

"I'll need to go shopping tomorrow. Big time. I have to replace my laptop, my camera, and all the other accessories in the camera bag. Unless that's still there?"

"Afraid not, Pip. But we can hit the mall first thing in the morning."

"We could, *if* the mall opened first thing?" I had to laugh. "The malls and big-box stores don't open until at least eleven on Sundays."

"Right, I forgot. Back east, things are always open."

He smiled again as he said it, and that smile caused a flutter in my stomach, which put me in a precarious position. I was holed up in a hotel room with my old nemesis, but he was now smoking hot and ticked every box I had—except I wasn't prepared to go there. Also, I had no idea if he was into me that way. So, ignoring my libido and without checking to make sure the sofa bed had linens, I grabbed my things, then headed into the bathroom to change. When I came out, I slipped between the satin sheets on the surprisingly comfy bed.

I'd hoped to go to sleep right away but falling asleep wasn't an easy feat as I suffered from insomnia. Typically, I crawled into bed and just lay there, eyes closed and waiting for sleep, which was why I heard Devon use his phone. Curious, I listened and caught him talking soft and low.

"Simon? Yeah." After a slight pause, Devon spoke again. "Got it." There was another pause. "Seems to be. I'll look into it."

He ended the call, and while what I overheard could be entirely innocent and meaningless in the big scheme of things, I wondered if something nefarious was going on. What if Devon wasn't who we all thought he was? I tried to tell myself to stop having such ridiculous thoughts, that Matilda certainly knew her own nephew. She'd raised him, and I grew up with him. Yes, Devon was annoying, but evil? No. There *was* something amiss, however, and I intended to find out what it was.

The following morning, there was no sign of Devon. Relieved, I decided to do my version of simple yoga and meditate before coffee. I threw on a t-shirt just in case because I didn't want a repeat of when I found him in my kitchen. As it turned out, his timing was impeccable. Just as I finished, he arrived bearing gifts from the bakery next door. There was no better way to butter me up than with croissants and coffee, and as the suite had a lovely little café table with two chairs, I didn't have to sit cross-legged on the bed to enjoy it all.

We checked out mid-morning and headed to the only mall near Luckland, about thirty miles away, but the tech store I shopped at most often was there. Usually, I went by myself, browsed around, used their online directory to search for things, and maybe asked a question or two. I liked to feel I knew my stuff. However, shopping with Devon was a whole new experience. The first thing I did when we entered the store was head straight for the laptop section, looking for my exact model. I didn't like change, and as I was already familiar with the one I had, I could recreate all my settings. Devon shook his head when he saw me checking out the display.

"That model doesn't have adequate security. You need fingerprint access or face recognition. Anyone could get into your old laptop."

Thanks for sharing that tidbit since anyone *was out there with my old laptop.*

"Look at this one, Pip. It'll autocorrect your photos while uploading."

I glared at him because I was *a photographer*. I didn't auto-correct.

"Careful with the remote access features!" he called out from somewhere in aisle five.

In the end, I wound up with Devon's laptop choice, but it would take me weeks to get used to all the new features. Luckily, he knew nothing about cameras, which meant I was free to wander about and choose my own. I was going to miss my old friend, but making new friends had its advantages. The one I found had Wi-Fi upload, so I didn't need to load the photos onto the laptop first. Big plus. I also took advantage of a two for one lens deal.

All in all, while I hit my savings account pretty hard, it was a good haul. Knowing my insurance would cover the cost helped ease the pain just a bit. Now all I wanted to know was when I'd be able to go home. There was no way I was going back to the Inn. By the time we got back to town, it was mid-afternoon, so we stopped at the sheriff's office to get their blessing to reenter my home and get back to my life.

CHAPTER EIGHT

WE ENDED UP AT MATILDA'S BECAUSE THE DEPUTIES WEREN'T QUITE ready for me to go back to my place. Matilda, gracious as always, provided me with a comfy blanket to hang out on the deck and fiddle with my new laptop. She also brought me a bottle of fabulous Pinot Noir, and once I settled on my favorite chair, which I'd warned Devon to stay away from, I finally relaxed.

"Hey, Red, check this out."

Just when I thought a little peace would be mine, Devon had to ruin it. "Check what out?"

"Our yearbook!"

Oh god, no. I did not want to take a trip down memory lane with Devon. As nerdy as he might have been in high school, I was extremely awkward. I hadn't *bloomed* like my best friend Dani, which meant the photos of me weren't as flattering. One, in particular, always made me cringe, and hoped Devon wouldn't see it.

He came right on over, pushed my legs off the side of the chair so he could sit—forcing me to grab my laptop before it slipped off—and began leafing through the pages.

"This is my favorite," he said, grinning. I was afraid to look —and groaned when I spotted the picture of me in my band uniform. Quite possibly the most embarrassing photo in existence. I was sitting on the bleachers in an ill-fitting jacket with shiny buttons down the front, tassels on the shoulders, and my red pigtails sticking out of a bizarre-looking hat with a feather on top.

"I never figured out who took that picture or how they sneaked it into the yearbook. Must have been one of my hundred or so admirers, right?" I looked at Devon, expecting him to laugh since we knew I wasn't a guy magnet in high school.

"Actually, Red, it was me." He said that with only a half-grin, unsure I would smile in return or run and get a butcher knife. I wasn't sure either.

"I don't get it."

"You never did." He slowly shook his head.

I got the strangest sensation I'd missed something. Or maybe, I wasn't ready to go searching for it. I purposefully took the book from him and flipped to my favorite photo. It was of Devon in the science lab, complete with his lab coat and goggles. I'd always loved that one. Of course, I was the one who took it.

"This is a classic." I grinned. Two could play at that game.

"There's more where this came from." Just like that, he took off into the house. A few minutes later, he came back out carrying a stack of memory books and handed them to me. Right on top was what looked like an old scrapbook with Matilda's sprawling signature across the front. I opened that one first.

The first page was adorable. A photo of four little girls, no more than seven or eight years old, in Easter dresses and carrying baskets. I turned to the next page to find an old clipping of Nixon resigning. The next few pages all featured photos of Matilda, my mom, Prudence, and Hope at various stages of their lives. There were a few local clippings as well. The time when a district TV station did a feature story on a group of gold seekers. Another clipping detailed how someone had tried to steal the alleged original map from the wall in the mayor's office. After that incident, the town council locked the map in a display case at the town hall. I browsed through a few more pages until another photo caught my eye.

The photo was of my mom and her besties in front of the Vegas sign. The one on my postcard. The best friends must have been around thirty, give or take, all smiles, posing for the camera. I wasn't sure what surprised me more—they were in Vegas or their hair. It was gigantic hair. Blown and teased like some eighties pop star. Getting that effect must have taken them hours.

"Well, holy cannoli," I exclaimed.

"What is it?" Devon tried to look over my shoulder. He was close. So close, I caught a hint of the mango-tangerine shower gel Matilda kept around for guests.

I moved aside so he could see. "The Luckland Ladies on a Vegas junket, who knew?" I didn't want to make a big deal of it, but in reality, it was a monstrous-sized deal. As far as I could remember, the only vacations they took were to the cabin located at the top of a mountain at the end of a long, private road. The cabin was actually a full-on house with six bedrooms, six baths, and a full gourmet kitchen. When we were kids, it was where we went for summers, weekends, birthdays, and anniversaries. The ladies considered the cabin their second home and the only place worth visiting. I honestly didn't think any of them had ever left the state of Colorado.

On the next page was a somewhat blurry photo of someone singing on a stage. I couldn't really see much and thought it was probably just a show of some sort. Beneath it was a folded piece of legal-looking paper. I started to unfold it, but Devon put his hand over mine to stop me.

"Leave that."

Curious, I glanced at him, but he'd shuttered his expression. I *could* have pushed him, but I doubted he'd budge. Instead, I carefully turned the scrapbook page to the next one. I looked at the aged and faded clipping then glanced at Devon, who frowned. I began reading aloud. "Casino Heist Nets Millions." The date said October eleventh, 1989. I flipped back to the previous page and checked the date stamped in the bottom right of the photo. October tenth, 1989. The day before. I turned to face Devon.

"Where, Professor Snooper, did you find this scrapbook? I've never seen it before. Have you?"

He hesitated. I think because he *had* been snooping. The sun was starting to set now, and the fading light made it hard to see, but I was sure guilt was written all over his face.

"No, I've never seen it before either. It was with the year-book." He reached for the scrapbook. "Let me see that."

"No. You gave it to me, and I'm not done with it." There was no way was I letting go.

"Okay, read it then," he said, his expression and tone childishly petulant. I would have smiled, but I doubted he'd know why.

"Las Vegas Police reported earlier today that two armed bandits robbed the Lazy Slot Casino in the first heist in a decade. The thieves reportedly got away with a cache of hundred-dollar bills stuffed into several large carpetbags. It's got a picture here of an old-school carpetbag. Look at this." I held it up so he could see.

"Carpetbags?" Devon looked skeptical.

"Why not? You know, once upon a time, in the days before

Bluetooth luggage, if you headed off for the weekend, you'd pack one of those funky-looking bags, usually made of fabric that looked like an area rug, and it had a clasp closure. It just snapped into place. No lock. No wheels. Only a handle to carry it." So far, I thought it a fascinating story, so I continued.

"Witnesses reported seeing the thieves atop the casino rooftop, and the police were on scene within minutes. A shootout with the burglars took place on the Las Vegas Strip. There were no injuries. However, the suspects are still at large." I glanced at Devon. "It happened around the same time as their visit, and she kept this article. Odd thing as a memento, but remarkably interesting, don't you think?"

"Turn the page."

Good grief, he sure was good at ordering people around. I did turn the page, though, and sucked in a breath at the photo of Hope and Prudence, sitting on a hotel bed, each with their hand on one side of...a carpetbag. That was not good. That was *so* not good. Eyes wide, I looked at Devon. His eyes were blazing, and he was staring right back, his expression filled with dread.

"Devon. Pippa. I'm heading out."

Devon and I looked up as Matilda popped out onto the deck. She dropped her gaze to the scrapbook on my lap, then shifted to stare at Devon. In an instant, she turned and legged it, which caught me by surprise because I'd never seen Matilda move faster than a snail's pace.

Devon jumped up. "Tillie, wait!" He started to go after her, but she turned and glared at him, putting her hand up like a stop sign. He stopped. I had a bad feeling about all this. I was sure he did too, but at that moment, letting her go seemed prudent. The garage door opened, then closed. Knowing she'd left, we looked at each other, digesting it all.

"You're thinking what I'm thinking, right?" I asked. Of course, he was.

"What *are* you thinking?" Just like that, the old Devon was back.

"You first." I was in no mood for games and wasn't sure about anything anymore. The possibility my mother was a criminal, a big-time thief, no less, made my head spin.

"Turn the page. Never mind." He sat back down, reached across, and turned it himself.

Another newspaper article. This one from 1999.

Cold case detectives back on the hunt for the Vegas Millions.

It appeared the FBI still searched for the money ten years later. Nothing like letting sleeping dogs lie.

"Let me see that," he said and grabbed the book out of my hands.

"Somebody needs to teach you some manners," I muttered.

I leaned over his shoulder to read the rest of the article. It mentioned some of the bills taken in the heist had turned up in various towns in Colorado. Right after the heist. That didn't bode well. However, the article also said bills had turned up in other places.

He flipped to the next page, where there was an even more recent article. Again, more details about the clues as to where the money might be but no resolution. I never saw Luckland mentioned, which would be a point in our favor, but Devon didn't look so sure. He also didn't appear surprised by any of this. He looked like a man on a mission.

"They're in this up to their eyeballs, aren't they?" I asked.

"We don't know that. Unless those shoeboxes are filled with cash, which might explain why they want them back."

Devon must have noticed I was on the verge of hyperventilating because he took my hand. "We don't know for certain, and we can't mention we know about the bagful of money to anyone. It might alarm the ladies, and I don't want to do that if I can help it. Let's find out a bit more first."

"How?"

"I'm an investigator. That's my job. So, let's go and talk to your dad."

"My dad?"

"If someone knows something, he might."

After I'd slowly extricated my hand because I wasn't comfortable with him holding it, we walked two doors down to my dad's house. "What if my mom sees us, she'll naturally come and join us. Then what will we do?"

"Not to worry, just follow my lead, Red." He gave me a reassuring smile.

"Roger, Dodger." I smiled, then took a deep breath for good measure. I was suddenly sure we were about to enter a very sticky situation.

"Pippa! Devon! What brings you here?" My dad beamed as he saw us, ushering us into the house, which was a mirror of my mom's but without the clutter.

"Well, we—"

"Have you eaten? I was just about to grill up a steak. Your mom's off with the girls. Book club. They're reading Emma."

I breathed a sigh of relief while Devon clapped my dad on the back. "A steak would be great, Colin, thank you. I'll help."

The two headed out to the backyard, which left me in the kitchen to contemplate being the daughter of a thief. It wasn't a nice thought. To distract myself, I made a pitcher of margaritas using the mix in the fridge, then took it out to the deck.

I poured each of us one, then tuned in to Dad and Devon's conversation. Sadly, the only discussion was about the proper way to determine whether the meat was still mooing or not. Maybe Devon was just warming up. I hoped so.

By the time the steaks were done, I was two margaritas in and ready for some answers. Chilly, we sat inside, then Devon turned to face my dad directly.

"Colin, have you ever been to Vegas? I know Pippa here hasn't, but I thought maybe you'd have gone a time or two."

"Me? Nah, not the type. The girls have though. That's where Kate had her bachelorette party. Bet she never told you about that, eh?" My dad winked at me, and I wondered how much he knew about that trip.

"Definitely not a story I've heard, Dad, but please, do tell!"

"Oh, it's not for me to tell. I wasn't there." He chuckled. "No men allowed. I know they had a heck of a time though."

I stole a glance at Devon, his expression contemplative. I hoped he had a better idea of getting information out of my dad because what we'd tried so far wasn't working.

"Must have been fun for them," Devon said. "So, my mom went as well?"

"Of course. I mean, Tillie and Vegas? She wasn't going to get left behind!" My dad smiled.

It took me a moment to digest what they'd said. Devon had just asked if his *mom* had gone to Vegas, and my dad had mentioned Tillie. Matilda. Referring to Tillie as Devon's mom wasn't so farfetched considering she'd raised him, but by my dad's ashen face, it wasn't a parapraxis.

Holy guacamole! Matilda wasn't Devon's aunt at all. She was his mom. I stole another glance at Devon, worried about how he would react to that bit of news.

He didn't seem surprised. In fact, he looked as if he'd known. I couldn't quite wrap my head around it, and I poured myself another margarita. Then I remembered the Vegas photos that were from October 1989. Devon's birthday was in July 1990. A few months before mine. I did the math. Devon was conceived at the same time as that trip. So much for the diplomatic corps and the kidnapping in the Congo. That story always did seem a little fishy.

Glancing at Devon again, I felt sorry for him. Even if he *had* known or at least suspected Matilda was his mom, to have verbal confirmation must still have been a shock. So, I poured him another margarita too.

"What do you know about my father?" Devon's voice was pretty even for a guy who'd just been hit with some rollicking news. My dad, however, looked petrified. After he'd kept that secret for thirty years, he hadn't just opened the proverbial bag and let the cat out—he'd tipped the bag upside down until the cat had a hissy fit and bolted.

"I'm sorry, Devon, I never knew him. Back then, it wasn't something anyone discussed." Dad seemed sincerely apologetic.

His expression thoughtful, Devon nodded. "I don't suppose you have any cookies, do you?"

I looked at him as if he'd gone a little mad. "Cookies? Why on earth do you want cookies?" Maybe the news about Matilda being his mom had hit him harder than I thought. Having that on top of learning the matriarchs of our families may have ripped off millions from a casino wouldn't be easy to digest. Still, we'd come here to find out if my dad knew something about the money. I mean, how could he not?

"Dad, forget the cookies for a moment. There's something I'm curious about."

"What's that, Punkin?"

"It's about the cabin. How exactly did you all pay for it?"

"She means thanks for dinner, Colin, and we've got to run!" Devon took my hand and practically yanked me out of the chair. He didn't let go until we reached the sidewalk.

"Care to explain the sudden exit?"

"He can't know that we know, Pip. In case he knows."

"Yes, but I wasn't giving anything away."

"I didn't want to take the chance. We'd already mentioned Vegas."

"And you think he might have made the connection? Okay, but what's with the cookies?"

"Since I don't smoke, I can't chew on a cigar. Cookies help me think."

Devon glanced at me and grinned. I couldn't help but grin back even as we headed back to Matilda's—thereafter to be known as Devon's mom's house.

CHAPTER NINE

Matilda hadn't yet returned home when we arrived, so Devon and I made ourselves comfortable in the living room. Devon lay lengthwise on the sofa, feet resting on the armrest at one end, head on the throw pillow at the other. In so many ways, he was not the boy I used to know. Not even a smidge. He was an enigma. I found myself trying to decipher his expression. He seemed more pensive than upset for someone who'd just discovered a nest of life-altering secrets. He caught me studying him.

"What are you thinking, Red?" he asked, his gaze open and direct.

"I'm wondering how long you've known Tillie wasn't just playing the role of your mom." Most guys I knew would have headed straight to the bar and downed a few pitchers after finding out their life's story was a lie.

"Let's just say there was a bit of confusion with a background check a while back," he answered, rather matter-of-fact. That was something I wouldn't have considered, though it did make perfect sense. I wanted to know more but felt it would be safer to talk about the mystery of the money and the shoeboxes.

"How about we talk about the other elephant in the room—the Vegas heist and whether the ladies had anything to do with it. Also, there's the postcard from Vegas that said, '*We know you took it, so give it back, or you will pay. Dearly.*'" I knew the damn thing word for word. "So, if we assume the ladies stole the money, and whoever sent the postcard wants the money back, that means...what?"

"That the ladies were in league with others? It's possible, but that doesn't explain why someone sent *you* the postcard and broke into your house."

"Oh, you think the break-in is linked to the postcard?"

"It's a distinct possibility, and I'm sorry I didn't mention it before now. Until we knew for sure, I didn't want to worry you or have you jump to the wrong conclusion. There have been a lot of tourists in town this week. There's still an infinitesimal chance the postcard and the break-in aren't connected."

I didn't know why I hadn't thought the two were connected. Probably, on some subconscious level, I didn't want to consider the possibility. "What if they know I'm Kate's daughter and thought threatening me would unsettle my mom? Maybe they assumed I'd show her the postcard, and she'd know what they meant. But then what? They'd contact her or me again? Perhaps breaking into my house *was* another message, one that's telling me, or Mom, they mean business."

"How did they know you're Kate's daughter? How did they make the connection?"

"They were watching me?" I shuddered as I said that. "Or they thought Kate lived in that house? There are a hundred scenarios, a hundred maybes. We can't go through them all."

Devon did that internal thinking thing of his I'd begun to recognize. "Who's your landlord?"

"I don't know. I go through a property management company."

"Then we need to find out." He grabbed his phone and began tapping furiously.

I held my breath, waiting to see what he found. My stomach flipped when his eyes went wide.

"What?" I whispered.

He looked at me and shook his head as if in disbelief. "That house was purchased in 1997 by the Luckland Women's Society."

"The who? I've never heard of them."

"It's a land trust. Want to know who the trustees are?"

At his expression, I didn't need him to tell me. I could figure it out on my own. I was a bit taken aback at the idea though. When I'd rented the little cottage a year earlier, it was to exert some independence. Have my own place to bunk when I came back to Luckland from my travels. My mother *found* the place for me. I should have known.

"I'm going to take a shot in the dark here. For argument's sake, let's say there isn't any Uncle Ernie or Aunt Lucy. I do have dead relatives, but we're not looking for boxes of lost souls, are we?"

He laughed at that. Good, he hadn't yet lost that ability.

"Good deductions there, Watson. The question is, what *is* in those boxes? Maybe they really do have the casino stash," Devon said.

"But the boxes were at my mom's. If the ladies had hidden the money in boxes, wouldn't they have divided them?"

"Yes, but we don't know that the boxes at your mom's were the only boxes, do we? Maybe more boxes exist."

"Okay, let's just say they came back home with oodles of cash," I said. "They stash it all in shoeboxes. Now clearly, they wouldn't keep it there for long. Think about it, Devon. They'd have to launder it. Isn't that what the mob does? Buy and sell stuff with the cash, so it disappears?"

I truly had Devon's attention at that point. It was kind of exciting if I ignored the fact we were now part of the dubious legacy of the Luckland Mafia.

Devon got up and started pacing. "It seems obvious they used the money to build the cabin. Also, none of us ever needed student loans. We all had 'school funds' and went to college debt-free. We all got cars when we passed our road tests. Another of those saving funds the ladies talked about. Funny, growing up, none of us questioned how fortunate we all were."

I noticed he spoke as if we were all offspring of the thieving women. As if it were perfectly natural for him to be Matilda's son—confirming he'd known for an awfully long time. *How* long was the question? I tucked that one away to ask him later.

The facts were clear. We'd all been living off the ill-gotten gains of a Vegas caper. It was a lot for me to digest. Our entire lives were suddenly straight off the big screen. It seemed Devon liked the idea about living off the stolen money as much as I did.

"Look, let's not assume anything. When Tillie gets home, we'll ask her," I said. If the apple didn't fall far from the tree, then being direct would work just as well with Matilda as it did with Devon.

"Just like that?" He looked skeptical.

"Just like that."

No sooner had I said that than in waltzed Matilda. A little too happy, it seemed to me. As flustered as she was when she saw us with the scrapbook, I would have thought she'd try to sneak in, but no, she just glided in and took a seat on the sofa, then patted the cushion, indicating to Devon that he needed to sit.

"Well now." Her tone indicated she'd had more than one drink that night. "It looks as if you found your birth certificate in the scrapbook, and I suppose you want to know more about your, shall we say, roots?"

Birth certificate? I glanced at Devon, who shook his head slightly as if warning me not to say anything. I frowned but gave him a slight nod, figuring I'd also pry that bit of information out of him later. However, the fact we'd discovered their million-dollar secret didn't seem to be Matilda's immediate concern. Instead, she was ready to talk bloodlines. I decided I ought to slip out. It seemed to be a very private conversation, but as I started to get up, she shooed me back down.

"No, Pippa, you stay. What involves one of us involves all of us."

"Tillie, how did you get home? You didn't drive, did you?" I seriously hoped she'd walked.

"Oh, no, luvvie. As you can see, I'm in no condition to operate heavy machinery. Speaking of, maybe one of you two dears could fetch me a drink. Some iced tea would be fine."

I let out a sigh of relief. One more drink, and she'd teeter over. I assumed that as soon as Devon and I had left my dad, he'd called her, which meant she was at least somewhat prepared to have this discussion.

Matilda waited for Devon to return with a pitcher of tea and some glasses pre-filled with ice. He set it all down on the coffee table in front of her, and she poured each of us a drink before serving herself. Most of the tea managed to make it into the glasses, which in her state was quite remarkable. Once we'd all settled back in, she cleared her throat.

"Well, now. Where to begin? I suppose, with an apology. I didn't mean to lie to you for all those years, but really, wasn't it better to have your parents carted off into the jungle than be the son of a Vegas crooner?"

Right there, I knew the story was going to be good.

"I don't know. Maybe I would have joined the choir had I

known." Devon smiled to let her know he wasn't upset, and she smiled in return.

"Well, as you now know, Kate's bachelorette party was in Vegas, and it was pretty wild. We ended up at this casino nightclub where we had too many drinks. Then this singer took the stage—a dead ringer for Jon Bon Jovi. Our eyes met, and we just connected. It was cosmic, really. Anyhoo, one thing led to another, and nine months later, you arrived." Matilda sat back and patted Devon's leg.

"Does Devon's father know? Did you tell him?" I asked, astonished.

"No. It didn't seem necessary. I mean, it was one night. He really was more of a sperm donor."

In all fairness to Matilda, that was kind of the prevalent attitude in the eighties. Thankfully, my generation referred to them as biological fathers with rights and obligations. Rightly so. I wondered if Devon would look him up.

I had to know one thing. "Tillie, can I ask who those people are in the photos on your wall?" Obviously, not Devon's parents.

"Why, I wouldn't know, dear. They came with the frames."

So, it seemed Matilda never had a brother or sister. Then how had she managed to get away with saying Devon was her nephew when most of the older generation in Luckland would have known she didn't have a sibling? That was a question I was never going to ask. I'd leave that up to Devon if he ever wanted to know.

I looked at him—just to make sure he was still okay. His easy and genuine smile told me he was fine. He took Matilda's hand in his and looked her in the eye.

"Well, truth is, they always looked a little stiff for my taste." He chuckled. "Really. It's all good. You finally told me the truth, and now we'll move on."

"Yes, but I really shouldn't have lied to you."

"Don't worry about it. Besides, it was a pretty good story. Props for that."

He glanced at me and winked. It was all very smooth but complete and utter bullshit. I'd bet he'd already ordered a DNA test and probably just waited on the results, but if his pacification helped make Matilda feel better, I was okay with it.

She patted his leg again, then stood and sighed. "If you kids don't mind, I'm going to get some sleep. Then we can all chat about this in the morning." She yawned, swayed a bit, and turned to go.

So much for interrogating her about the money.

We let her take her leave, as she liked to put it, then Devon and I sat for a few minutes longer, letting it all seep in. To be honest, it had been a monstrously chaotic weekend, and I was exhausted. I supposed we both were. Then Devon came over and pulled me out of the chair.

"Come on, Red, let's call it a night."

I faced him, eying him nervously. For one brief moment, I wondered if this was headed in a very perilous direction. It seemed the more time we spent together, the more time I wanted to spend with him. Just the touch of his hand in mine was electrifying. Logically I knew he was just helping me up. Nothing else. I just didn't know whether I was relieved or disappointed he hadn't leaned in for a kiss or asked me to go to his room or...

Thankfully, the spare bedroom at the top of the stairs was ready and waiting, for which I was grateful. At least I could have some solitude to play everything back in my mind as I endlessly waited to fall asleep.

CHAPTER TEN

I PROBABLY WOULD HAVE SLEPT UNTIL NOON HAD MY PHONE NOT started buzzing like a chainsaw. It was a text frenzy from Babs, who ordered me to go to Mom's house immediately. There was an emergency. *Not again.*

I now had to hurry and get dressed, have coffee, then walk over to my mom's, who lived next door. All the ladies lived on the same street within shouting distance of one another, but I was simply not in the mood for any Babs drama. I needed to work on my article "The Meadow Bloom." Not that it was a priority at that particular moment. I could name a dozen more important things, but the article was certainly a much-needed distraction. However, on the minuscule chance there really was another emergency, I decided to get up and deal with it.

My bleary-eyed self found Devon waiting in the kitchen with a million-dollar smile and a fresh cup of coffee, which I had to admit was a sight for sore eyes, but as I drank the elixir of life, Devon began to mess with my phone. "What are you doing, Dev? Stealing more photos?" I hadn't yet confronted him about stealing them the first time.

"Nope. Just loading an app on your phone. With all that's going on, I want to make sure you're safe."

"You do?"

"Yeah, Red, I do." He handed me back the phone. "So, if you ever need my help, just hit the emergency button."

"I don't have an emergency button." At least I wasn't *familiar* with any emergency button on my phone.

He reached over and tapped my screen, then pointed to a new little icon that looked like a caution sign. "Just push it. That's all. I'll be there in a flash." He seemed so sincere it took me unawares.

"Is that a PI thing?" I realized if he used something like that, he must work with others. Maybe that Simon guy Devon was on the phone with at the Inn. "Tell me something, Mr. super techno-geek. How did you unlock my phone? It's got a password."

"Pippa, don't you know not to use personal info for your PIN? You need to use the fingerprint sensor."

"Please, that never works. Try using that when you've got lotion on your hands or when your fingers are wet." His face took on that horrified expression that had started to grow on me.

"Do you *want* anyone to get into your phone?" By anyone, I assumed he meant himself, and clearly, my answer would be no way in hell.

He stood there like a drill sergeant until I set up my phone to unlock with not one but four different fingers. He also had me change the PIN to an unlock pattern. I held up my phone in triumph once I'd finished. "Guess you won't be snooping in my private conversations anymore."

He shook his head and laughed, which was definitely not a good sign. Nor was my reaction to the rich baritone of his laughter. Devon Marks was a handful.

I arrived at my mom's to find a meeting of the Luckland Ladies already in session. Prudence, Hope, my mom, and Matilda. Even Babs. They were all sitting outside at the table on the patio and looking at me intently as I scraped my chair on the concrete before I sat. "What?" I looked around the circle of women.

The posse all looked at each other... Actually, they gave each other *that* look. The silent message. The slight nod. The smirk. Their attitude was absurd and not tolerable at that hour.

"Out with it," I said. "Did I grow warts on my nose? Is my shirt inside out?"

Babs tipped her head. "You still haven't, have you?"

"Haven't what?"

Prudence smiled. "We were hoping you and Devon might have, you know..."

The idea that these grown women were sitting around discussing my sex life was disturbing, so of course, my mind headed in the one direction I'd been blocking for three days. *Nope. Still not going there.*

"Ladies, you really need to mind your own affairs, no pun intended, and stay out of mine." I smiled to take the sting out of my words. "Seriously, he's been here less than a week. Not that I have any interest anyway." I threw that in for good measure, even if it became more evident by the hour that it was a bald-faced lie. I gave each one of them a very deliberate look. My best, *don't you dare* look. They all just glanced at one another again and gave a collective sigh.

"I really hope this wasn't your emergency." I didn't think it was, but it was hard to tell with that bunch.

"Don't be ridiculous, Pippa," my mom said. "This is serious business. The girls and I have something to discuss with you and Barbara. Now. Let's get to it." She sat back and waved at

Hope, indicating she should be the one to start things off. Unfortunately, Hope would make it a long, long tale.

"As you girls know, your mother, Matilda, Prudence, and I, have been friends for a very long time. Now, when your father proposed to your mother, we were all over the moon. We adored your father, you know. Who wouldn't? Since Pru was recently single and I hadn't yet met Marcy, we decided right away we wanted to have one last fling. Just the four of us. A real bachelorette party. However, back then, Luckland really wasn't the place to let loose, as they say. I think you now call it getting lit. Anyhoo, Pru suggested we all go to Las Vegas, stay at one of those fancy hotel casinos, and perhaps tie one on."

Now I was all ears. I glanced at Babs, who leaned forward in her chair.

"To be clear, girls, your mother was really quite well-behaved. No debauchery or table dancing. That was Matilda's forte." That elicited a few snickers around the table. Then they were all talking at once. Matilda defended herself. Prudence described the whole lounge singer event. My mother ventured off to la-la land, remembering it all, I supposed. Hope just gave everyone her librarian look and waited for silence so she could go on.

"As I was saying. Tillie had a little more fun than the rest of us that first night. She took one look at the lounge singer belting out one of those hairband love ballads so popular back then, and she was totally gaga. After his last set, and a few shots of some oddly named liquor—oh, Pru, what was that called? Never mind, anyway—Tillie ran off to have some fun with him." I really liked Hope's version better than Matilda's.

"Tillie, really? A lounge singer!" My sister's tone was just a tad judgmental. I waited to see how Matilda would react.

"Honestly, Barbara, it was worth it. You see, that's how I got my Devon, who, by the way, looks just like him. Total Jon Bon Jovi look-alike."

I had never seen Babs look quite so shocked about anything. She had that knocked in the head by a coconut kind of expression. I honestly hadn't thought about the genetics, but if that guy in Vegas looked anything like Devon or Jon Bon Jovi, I would have done just what Matilda had, so mine was a judgment-free zone.

After a minute or two, Babs nodded. "Go on."

"Oh, let me tell the next part," Prudence said, jumping in. "The next night, we had a wonderful dinner and a show, and thanks to Tillie's amazing voice, polished off a bottle or two of complimentary Champagne. Prosecco wasn't a thing back then. It was either sparkling wine or the real deal. Did you know you can't call it Champagne unless the grapes technically come from a particular region in France?"

I did, but I wasn't going to say so because I wanted her to finish the story.

"So, we're headed back to our hotel in a fabulous mood, still singing and holding each other up a bit. Then, suddenly we hear firecrackers. Well, we thought they were firecrackers. You know, Pop. Pop. Pop. Pop. We heard all this commotion and shouting."

"*'Stop! That way! Two of them! Look for the bags! They've got ski masks on!'*" Hope was up on her feet, agitated, her voice slightly frantic as she reenacted the scene. "When we heard all these people yelling, we realized they weren't firecrackers at all. They were gunshots. And there we stood, frozen in place on the sidewalk, which was all lit up by streetlights and searchlights, plus all those neon signs. You know the ones, flashing nudie girls and triple x."

"I thought we were all going to die." Matilda spoke quietly, almost as if she were right back there in time. "We grabbed each other and ran for our lives. I tell you, if I'd run that fast in gym class, I would have been the star of the track team, if we had had one."

Okay, so it looked as if they hadn't stolen the money. Devon and I had gotten it all wrong. How, then, did they end up with it?

My mother cleared her throat. "Now, girls, what I'm going to tell you next must never leave this patio. You cannot tell a soul." She looked directly at me. "Especially not Devon."

"Wait, what? Devon, the hero you brought in to save the day and find the boxes, can't *know* any of this?" Actually, didn't they realize he already knew about the money? Matilda had caught us looking through the scrapbook with all the information on the Vegas heist.

"Just promise me, Pip. Okay?"

I didn't want to agree because I was kind of hook, line, and sinker on Devon, which was not easy to admit, but it was also obvious wires had gotten crossed in some way, and I was curious to find out what they thought they needed to keep secret. So, I nodded.

Satisfied, she continued. "We had turned so many corners, blindly running until we found ourselves in a dark alley some-where. That was when I noticed Hope had a large bag in her hand. Probably why I found myself tugging her along the whole time. Right, Hope?"

Hope nodded. "We were on the sidewalk before the ruckus began, and I felt as much as heard a loud thump next to me. I almost tripped over the bag when we heard the shots, so I picked it up and started running."

"Anyway," my mom said. "When we got back to the hotel, we went upstairs, shut the door, and locked it. Then we put a chair under the doorknob as a precaution." She looked at me as if I needed further explanation. "I'd seen that on TV."

"I grabbed the bag from Hope and put it on one of the beds," Matilda whispered before she glanced around. "We all sat and just stared at it for a moment. It was stuffed full; that much was clear. Also, quite heavy. Good thing Hope could carry it, though I'm still not sure how."

"I'm not either. I suppose it was adrenaline," Hope declared.

I found myself unable to keep my mouth shut. "Who opened it? What was in it?"

"Yes, yes, Pip, just getting to that," my mom replied. "I opened it. Wasn't even locked, for goodness' sake." She paused for dramatic effect. "It was crammed with stacks and stacks of money."

"Hundred-dollar bills, all of them," said Prudence.

"We had to count it, naturally," Matilda stated.

"Two million, five hundred and seventy thousand dollars to be exact," said Hope. "Which adjusted for inflation would be the equivalent of about seven million today."

"How did that all fit in one bag?" I asked after I figuratively picked myself up off the floor. Math wasn't my strong suit.

"Pippa, honey, a stack of hundred-dollar bills is ten thousand dollars, but it's only half an inch thick. The bag had exactly two hundred and seventy-five stacks of bills, which fit quite nicely in the bag. The bag was very neatly packed, by the way." Hope smiled triumphantly as if the neatness scored extra points.

"So, where's the money now? It's not in the shoeboxes, is it?" I looked at Babs, who had lost all color.

"Of course not. It's invested, dear," Matilda said.

That was certainly a relief and as much as Devon and I suspected. "And where is it invested?"

"Well, that's the thing, dear," said Hope. "We chose to diversify."

"She means it's all over the place," Prudence explained.

"Mostly, we invested in shares."

"We have funds deposited into our bank accounts every month for each of us," my mother said. "But because all the *information* about the money is in those boxes, we must get them back."

"If someone were to find those boxes, they'd know where all the money is," Babs said. Some color had returned to her face. "And they could trace it back."

"Exactly, Barbara, my dear. We found millions of dollars. Millions. Obviously, somebody would come looking for it someday, so we have to guard that information," Prudence declared.

It was pretty clear why the ladies all acted desperate to find those boxes. I was now desperate to find them too. "We need to tell Devon. He needs to know what he's looking for," I said.

"No, Pippa. You must not let him know. I thought we made that clear?" My mother was adamant, but so was I.

"You brought him into this and asked him to find the boxes. He's doing his best, but if you withhold information, he can't possibly get them back. That's not very fair."

The ladies refused to budge—just gave one another their signature secretive looks.

"Don't you trust him? Is there something else going on?" I asked.

"Just for once, Pip, keep this to yourself. We have our reasons."

I could tell I wouldn't get them to change their minds regarding Devon, but at least they hadn't stolen the money. Well, at least not from the casino. However, keeping Devon in the dark about that didn't sit right. He needed to know the truth, but I didn't think I knew what the truth was—at least not all of it. For instance, why tell Babs and me about the money now? There had to be something else the ladies were keeping secret.

CHAPTER ELEVEN

"Now, about the emergency." My mother stood and began to pace.

"Wait. What? I thought the missing boxes with all that money laundering info *was* the emergency." *How bad could this get?*

"Oh no, that's merely an incidental crisis," Hope said.

"Quite so, the emergency is regarding last night's book club," said Matilda. "I'm sure you wondered why I was three sheets to the wind last night."

"I thought that was because we discovered your secret about Devon being your son." It was obvious to me now that she hadn't realized Devon and I had found the newspaper clippings about the Vegas heist and the picture of all of them with the carpet bag. She must have thought we'd stopped going through the scrapbook after finding his birth certificate—which I still had to ask him about.

"Water under the bridge, my girl," Matilda replied. "So many years ago, and all that. No, no, this is much worse. Someone is blackmailing us."

Before I had a chance to react, Marcy came outside. Tall and buxom—which I didn't think was a word anyone used anymore —she favored bold colors and eclectic garments, and she always wore a large pendant made from glass and shells. "This setup is all wrong. We need to move this inside."

With that, everyone followed her back into the house except Babs and me. We simply looked at each other for a moment, perhaps trying to second-guess what was going on. Ultimately, we had no choice but to head inside—where we found them all cross-legged on the floor in a circle.

"Mother, I demand to know what is going on. Who is black-mailing you, and why in god's name are you all sitting on the floor?" Babs said it all so fast she had to catch her breath. My sister rarely expressed anger. She was the quintessential willowy blonde who tended to mask any depth of emotion. Unless it was drama queen time.

The women stared up at us, eyebrows raised in apparent invitation. Since we were still standing, Prudence made the verbal request.

"Butts down on the floor, girls. Now." Commanded by Pru, Babs and I joined the circle on the floor, which was when I noticed the Tarot cards in front of Marcy.

"While I love a good game of cards, you can't just throw the word blackmail out there and not elaborate. So, someone had better explain," I said, making my tone quite firm.

Hope cleared her throat. I looked at her, and seriously, it was hard not to laugh. She had dressed in a pencil skirt and blazer, yet somehow could sit on the floor and still appear lady-like. If I had worn that outfit, I'd have ripped the side seam before even hitting the floor. She also had a neat little braided bun thing going with her hair, which at the time was a pretty, golden sunflower color. Hope tended to change her hair color often. She'd told me she used a rinse-in rinse-out color so her hair could match her mood.

"Last night, during book club—we're reading Emma, you know—Matilda's phone rang. Normally, we ask all participants to silence their phones." Hope gave Matilda her librarian look, then continued. "Anyhoo, she answered the phone, which is frowned upon, and suddenly she turned quite pale. We all knew something terrible had happened. At least that was our assumption."

"It was not terrible, just a bit of a shock," Matilda said. "It was your father, girls, informing me the moment I knew would eventually arrive, did."

I guessed that was the Devon birth reveal call, and Babs and I nodded in understanding, though I didn't understand what that had to do with someone blackmailing them.

Hope continued. "After Tillie told us what had happened, we had a drink or two. Maybe three. For us, this was a long time coming. We'd always known that someday it would happen. So, when Tillie's phone rang again, we assumed it was Devon, didn't we?"

The women all nodded and murmured their assent.

Matilda spoke up then. "Only it wasn't. It was a strange, muffled voice. Very threatening too. It said, 'I know your secrets.' I hung up the phone and was about to tell the girls when Hope's phone rang."

"Did you get the same threat?" Babs asked.

"Yes," said Hope. "Then, after I'd hung up, Kate's phone rang."

I looked at my mom, alarm now filling my chest. She nodded. "The same," she said.

We all turned to look at Pru. "I let my phone go to voicemail, then we all listened to see if we could discern who the voice belonged to."

"And did you?" I asked.

"No, not a clue," Matilda said. "But whoever it was sounded sinister."

"The fact is, whoever has the shoeboxes, opened them," said Hope. "And whoever it is, wants to destroy us."

I shook my head, trying to understand what they were saying. At least I now knew what prompted them to tell Babs and me about the money and what was in the boxes. I looked at Babs, who simply sat there, staring wide-eyed at the women— as if doing so would make it all go away.

"So, whoever opened the boxes found out about the money, and that's what they're threatening you with, right?" she asked.

"No, not just that. Everything *else*," Prudence said.

"What else could you possibly have to hide?" I didn't think I could take any more. My brain was all but fried. The ladies suddenly turned tight-lipped, and no amount of prodding would get them to tell me, but it seemed there were more secrets in those boxes that were worse than proof of over two million dollars of stolen money. "So let me get this straight. You asked Devon to find the shoeboxes, but you won't tell him what's inside, even though someone is blackmailing you regarding the contents."

"Yes," Matilda said. "He can't know anything."

I wanted to protest, but I'd already made a promise. "So, what are you going to do?"

"We'll let Marcy work her magic," my mom said.

I glanced at Marcy. "Magic?"

"To find out where the boxes are. Time is of the essence." Marcy shuffled the Tarot cards and looked at each of us. She directed her gaze back to me.

"Pippa, please place your hands lightly over the deck."

"Me? Why me?"

"Because, Pip, the cards are calling you. I have to let the Tarot guide us."

I looked around suspiciously but accepted that whatever Marcy said was law in the realm of Tarot. I put my hand on the deck.

"Now, concentrate, and ask the first question that pops into your head."

"Who's blackmailing you all?" I asked. Obviously, that was the question of the moment. Then Marcy nodded at me to lift my hands and cut the deck.

"We need to find out who it is, and quickly," she whispered as she turned over the first card.

CHAPTER TWELVE

The Tarot reading may have been a way to throw Babs and me off track, but I couldn't decide.

Marcy flipped over three cards and laid them face up. Everyone suddenly started oohing and aahing. Clearly, they'd done this before. I waited for an explanation, and when none came, I glanced at Babs, who seemed just as baffled.

"An interesting turn of events, I must say!" Marcy exclaimed.

My mother looked at me and shook her head. "I knew it," she said with a sigh and a weird hint of a smile. I scrutinized the women in the circle. Except Babs, they were all nodding at one another and grinning deviously.

I had to interject. "Hello? Care to explain? Who's blackmailing you?"

"Oh, my dear, we have no idea who's blackmailing us. It appears the real question on your mind concerns your love life," Marcy replied with an all too familiar smirk.

"My love life? What about it?" Thrown off course, I examined the cards, though I had absolutely no idea of their meaning.

"Oh, no time to explain now. We need to get moving!" With that, they all jumped up, which was no small feat for any of them. Then gathering their things, they said their goodbyes and were out the door in a flash. Babs, too, the traitor.

A little flustered with their abrupt departure, and by everything I'd learned, I headed back to Matilda's and found Devon at my laptop. Again.

"Okay, secret agent man, what are you doing with my laptop?"

"You didn't set up the security login as I told you to," he said without looking up—as if that made breaking into my laptop okay. It didn't. With a sigh, I decided getting some information about the man disrupting my life would be better than starting an argument.

"Tell me, Lone Ranger, where exactly did you ride in from? As in, where is home now?"

He seemed to contemplate that for a moment—wondering should he tell me or not. Then he glanced at me. "Virginia."

Oh. Virginia was kind of far, which would be a good thing if I were contemplating a short fling with him, but a short fling with Devon wasn't going to fly. In every fiber of my being, I knew a relationship with Devon would have to be all in or nothing at all.

"Say, Devon, can you maybe finish up on there and give me a ride home to get my Jeep?"

He smiled. "Of course. Give me a minute."

As I waited for Devon, I wondered if the fearless foursome had any idea how hard it would be to keep my mouth shut about the blackmail and what was in those boxes. I at least needed to tell him the ladies had found the bag of cash and had nothing to do with the Vegas heist—after all, it wasn't as if he didn't already know about the money. Torn, I decided to wait a little longer. As a PI, Devon might even figure it out on his own, which meant I could keep my promise to my mother. What frustrated me was that Devon was one of us and the investigator to boot. It seemed counterintuitive to exclude the one person who might help fix everything.

On the way over to my house, I pushed my hands under my legs to hide their nervous shake. I had never been a victim of criminal activity before—Luckland just didn't have any measurable crime to speak of. Saying that, my mother insisted Babs and I took self-defense classes when we'd turned thirteen. Devon took those classes too. As our instructor was also the town's swimming and wrestling coach, we had never questioned it. Looking back, and considering the ladies were stashing millions of stolen bills, it kind of made sense, and I wondered whether the sudden crime spree was linked to their shady past or merely coincidence. Was it just a sign of the times that crime had found us all in Luckland?

The crime scene tape still lay across my front door. I wasn't able to go in yet, but the sheriff's office gave me the okay to have my Jeep, which was the same as having my freedom. Devon waited for me to check the back seat for any wayward humans, then after I started the engine, he waved and took off.

I headed to the shop, needing to immerse myself in a familiar and safe place. As usual, Dad greeted me with a hug, and I decided to see if he knew about the blackmail.

"So, Dad, did Mom mention anything unusual to you recently?" I asked.

He frowned. "Unusual? In what way?"

So, it seemed she hadn't told him about the threatening phone calls. "Oh, nothing specific, but I was with her this morning, and after Marcy drew some Tarot cards, the whole posse disappeared. I wondered if you knew what they were up to."

"Well, I don't know if they're up to anything, but your mom

has been a little distracted. I assumed it had something to do with that new auction lot she recently purchased."

I nodded, not wanting to alarm him or outright tell him his wife had more secrets and hidden depths than either of us had realized. "That must be it," I said, then I dragged my ass over to the little table I used as a desk and spent some time on my blog. Unfortunately, my mind kept drifting to the Tarot cards and Marcy's explanation of why the cards were about my love life and not who was supposedly blackmailing the ladies. Apparently, my love life, or perhaps the lack thereof, was the real question on my mind. I shook my head. By the women's reactions, they seemed to believe the cards involved Devon. The problem with that type of "divine knowledge" was that it planted ideas in people's heads. Expectations. I had an expectation of my own—they'd be disappointed. Though I couldn't deny I found Devon attractive, there were too many issues between us, not least because he was, well...*Devon.*

After a couple of hours, just as I'd finished sorting out which photos I wanted to use for my blog, my phone buzzed.

Devon: All clear. You can go home.

I stared at the message wondering why he couldn't have called me. Then I realized I hadn't put his information in my phone, which meant he'd put it there—which begged the question of what else he'd done to my phone.

I drove to my place with some trepidation, then released an enormous sigh of relief. Devon's sedan sat in my driveway, and he sat on my porch with no crime scene tape in sight. It was just what I needed. Whether it was reassurance that all was well or something else, I couldn't quite say. I just knew it felt right.

He stood as I approached, palm out, silently asking for the key. Not wanting any more surprises, I gave it to him, perfectly willing to let him go in first. I followed to find my home as neat as a pin—it was never that clean. Somebody had played fairy godmother.

"My mom was here?"

He looked quite taken aback, then laughed before shaking his head.

"Then, who?" I asked.

He smiled softly, his expression a little nervous. That was when I realized he'd done it himself. That was why he wanted me to come home.

"You?"

"Me." He tipped his head and looked at me questioningly. "It's okay, right? I mean, you like it?"

"I like it, Dev. It's perfect. How did you manage this?"

"I called the sheriff after I'd dropped you off and asked if they'd finished. He sent the deputy over for some last-minute cleanup, and she gave me the key."

"Devon, why would she give *you* the key?"

His expression turned sheepish. "I told her I wanted to surprise you."

"Thank you. I really appreciate all this. To also say thank you, if you haven't already spotted them, the cookies are in the top cupboard on the right of the fridge."

He laughed again, then took my hand and pulled me toward a flashy new panel on the wall next to the front door. After a couple of seconds of me staring at it, he explained it was all part of some hi-tech security system he'd put in place. Then he loaded yet another new app on my phone, so now I had two emergency icons—one to "call Devon to the rescue" and one for the alarm system.

"How did you get all this done? When the Wi-Fi is on the fritz, it takes at least forty-five minutes just to get the voice response system, known as customer service, on the phone."

"Someone owed me a favor." He shrugged as if it were no big deal.

I was just about to thank him again when a big, white, fluffy cat came trotting over, then plopped down in front of my feet before looking up at me expectantly.

"And who is this adorable feline?" I asked. Luckily, I wasn't allergic.

"Her name, according to the helpful woman at the adoption center, is 99." He smiled, then waited to see if I got it. I did and smiled back. I might have looked a bit goofy, but the situation was a bit off the rails. Plus, the significance of 99 wasn't lost on me; she was a secret agent in Get Smart. One of my favorite movies.

"She's three years old, and her owner has passed on, so she needs a new home. I figured you're alone here, and she could keep you company." It was a long-winded explanation for a perfect gift. I didn't mind. I crouched and gave her the belly rub she expected. She purred so loudly I assumed we were getting off to a good start—until she abruptly got up and rubbed against Devon's legs. Well, that simply proved she was a suck-up.

"Did you bring supplies for her?"

"Yup! Litter, check. Food, check. Water bowl, check. Comb and brush combo, check."

"Okay," I said with a laugh. "I get it." I hadn't had a cat since Ms. Fluffy. Babs and I were so distraught when she finally succumbed to old age that neither of us ventured to get another cat. I supposed it was time to move on, and 99 sure looked like a good fit.

"How about I make some lunch, and you can relax. Perhaps take your new camera out to the backyard," Devon said, a little out of the blue.

"Oh, well. I was thinking of taking a quick hike."

"A hike? Pip, I know I sometimes seem a bit bossy, but it's not safe for you to go on a hike alone. Not right now. Whoever broke in here is out there."

"I realize that, but getting out onto the hills is the best way to clear my head, and after everything that's recently happened, I need to de-stress."

I figured Devon would outright tell me to stay home, but he stepped closer to me and gently grasped my hand. "I understand, I do, but I'd feel so much better if you wouldn't put yourself in such a vulnerable position. We don't know if anyone is still watching you."

"If anyone is," I said.

Devon tipped his head to acknowledge of my statement but tightened his fingers on mine. "It's not a chance I'm willing to take. You can take photos here to relax, right?"

He looked awfully serious. I hated that the place I'd always thought of as my safe haven perhaps wasn't safe anymore, and I hated that some intruder was depriving me of my right to do something I loved, but Devon was right. My safety was more important than my need to get my head on straight. Reluctantly, I nodded.

"I'll make lunch," he said with a smile.

I had no idea how long I was outside, but when Devon called from the back door that lunch was ready, I didn't hesitate to take a break. I tended to get caught up in my work and forgot about meals, so having someone prepare lunch was a luxury. I imagined Devon ate on a more regular basis, and he sure didn't get all that muscle tone from rabbit food.

He'd set the table with plates, silverware, glasses, and a pitcher of iced tea. There was a great big salad in the middle of the table—and not the twigs and leaves kind either. The salad had peppers, mushrooms, and heirloom tomatoes. Next to the salad sat a platter with an array of meats and cheeses.

"What have we got here?" I leaned over to get a closer look at the selection.

"Charcuterie. Know what that is?"

I looked up to find him grinning. I didn't bother answering, just raised an eyebrow.

"Trust me. You'll love it."

"Where did you get all this?" Luckland didn't exactly have a gourmet grocer, and it sure as hell hadn't come from *my* kitchen.

"Just try it," he said as if he thought I was afraid. He must have misinterpreted my expression because I had no qualms about trying any of it. It was time to remind him who he was dealing with.

"So, there's this little wine bar in Paris, Le Barav." I popped a small slice of soppressata in my mouth. "Fabulous charcuterie. Been there?" I asked with a grin.

"Touché." He raised his glass toward me and laughed. "Paris, eh? When?"

"Summer after I graduated. Dani and I went. Not just Paris, but Geneva and Montreux, during the Jazz Festival, of course. Good excuse to use all that French we studied. Ever been?"

"Can't say I have. I did spend a bit of time in the UK, mostly London. I made a few trips to the Highlands as well."

That was an interesting tidbit. I didn't remember Matilda ever mentioning that, but considering the way she'd kept secrets, there was probably a lot about Devon she hadn't told anyone, which reminded me...

"Devon, I need to ask this. That birth certificate Matilda mentioned she had in the scrapbook? That was the piece of paper you didn't want me to open, wasn't it? Did you already know what it was?"

Devon nodded. "I guessed."

"So how long have you known, truthfully? It's just you're

awfully calm about it. Maybe calm isn't the right word. Maybe you're just settled with it." I waited, afraid if I pushed any further, I might push too far.

"Well, my line of work generally requires a lot of background and credential checks. I was gathering up all my documentation and realized I needed my birth certificate. The copy I had wasn't an official one with a seal. It listed what I suppose was that lovely couple hanging on the wall as my parents." He smiled and shook his head. I smiled back in encouragement. "When I ordered my actual certificate, I got a notice that my information didn't match the records. I wasn't sure what to do. I called the vital records office, and they politely suggested perhaps I was adopted, and if I was uncomfortable asking for the information, I could do a birth records search using just my name and birthdate. That's how I found out. I certainly didn't know the story behind it. It's quite a classic, don't you think?" He smiled. A warm, open smile that spoke volumes.

"You're a good son, Devon. Truly." I sincerely meant that. Treating Matilda with the dignity and respect she deserved unmasked a new layer to Devon I wasn't expecting. "Do you know who he is? Or is that overstepping?"

"I do, but she doesn't know how much I know, so it's not fair for me to tell you. I'll tell her when the time is right."

"*More* secrets. I don't do secrets very well."

He grinned. "We all know that, Pippa. It's part of your charm. So why don't you tell me about the emergency meeting? Was it about the money?"

It didn't take a deductive mind to figure Devon was fishing for information, and I sighed. "Kind of, but I promised I wouldn't tell you. I'm just not sure why they don't want you to know. I tried to explain it would be best for you to have all the information, but they said no."

"Okay, that's interesting."

"Interesting? It's wrong."

The light in Devon's green-blue eyes told me he might have meant it was interesting that I'd tried to get the ladies to tell him their secrets. A little smile touched his mouth, and I once again felt that flutter in my stomach. "Okay, I can tell you they didn't steal the money from the casino. The ladies found the carpetbag and dragged it to their hotel room."

"So, they told you about the money, but they told you not to tell me because they don't know I already know about it? Correct?"

"Yes. I think Matilda didn't realize what we saw in the scrapbook. She must have assumed we saw the birth certificate and nothing more."

"That makes sense. So why did the ladies tell you about the money after all this time?"

"That's what I can't tell you." I winced at having to keep such a secret. It really wasn't right, but until I knew *why* they didn't want Devon to know, it would be best I didn't say anything.

"Okay, I get it, but I'm a patient guy, Pip. Eventually, you'll tell me. Right?"

All I could do was nod slightly—not a full nod, more of a hesitant tip of my head, but it seemed it was enough, for now.

We spent the next few hours in a sort of hangout mode. We set up a little perimeter on the porch for 99 so she could be with us outside. While I fiddled with the camera, Devon followed me around intermittently, chatting about nothing and asking technical questions about what I was doing. It was tough to hold a discussion where he asked me if I liked chocolate or vanilla one minute, and the next, he asked what aperture I used. No one talked that way. He was still a nerd, but one I was growing very, very fond of.

As I watched him with 99, I realized I didn't know all that

much about him after he'd left Luckland. The things Matilda had said about him had been a little abstract, and I was sure there had to be more. "So, Matilda mentioned you were dating a model. Anyone I've heard of?" I thought that was a fair place to start, and he'd seemed willing to talk about himself earlier.

"I doubt it, Pip."

Damn, he was back to being evasive. "Well, what did she model? High fashion? Casual wear? Swimsuits?" I smiled and wiggled an eyebrow, hoping it came off flirty rather than awkward.

"As I said, I doubt you'd have seen her work."

I could tell I'd failed at the brow wiggle by the smirk he wore. "I might surprise you, so clue me in."

His smirk broadened. "Lotions and the occasional ring."

"Wait, she was a hand model?" I did everything I could not to laugh. I had done a few of those photo shoots myself. I was definitely going to discuss that whopper with Matilda later on. Talk about a bait and switch in the gossip department.

"Still dating? Or are you single now?" I held my breath a little as I waited for him to answer, though I wasn't sure why.

"Single. I guess I move around a lot, which isn't really conducive to a relationship."

I wondered at the regret I heard in his voice. I didn't date locally, and I didn't date long-term. I tended to have my best relationships while traveling. They would end right from the start, which meant I was free to be myself and walk away with my heart intact. I never wanted to entangle myself with anyone because I didn't want to get hurt. From my very first crush, I was the girl who ended up crushed. Babs was the one who attracted all the boys, and I was their go-to confidante. Though looking back, there was one exception. Devon. He'd never paid much attention to Babs at all.

"Having traveled a bit myself, I get that." I kept my reply

neutral while trying to come up with another question. Before I could, he smiled.

"I assume you're single now," he said.

"What makes you *assume* that?" I doubted Devon assumed anything. He probably knew for certain, and I knew how.

"Well, er." A flush colored Devon's cheeks before he grinned again. "They might have mentioned it when they told me to come home."

"Did they, now?" By *they,* he meant the busybody women.

"Yeah, I suppose I should tell you what else they said."

"I suppose you should," I said, though I was suddenly a bundle of nerves.

"They may have mentioned you were having a hard time getting over your last breakup. That you were still hurting." He looked quite concerned.

"Um, that would be a no." I inwardly chuckled because the women had told another whopper. None of them knew if I'd had any long-term relationships or whether I was actively dating. I never talked about my love life with anyone but Dani. Not even with my mother. The Luckland posse had clearly made up a story for his benefit.

"That's good to hear," he said with a soft smile. Then he reached over and tucked a stray curl behind my ear. He pulled back, and I couldn't do anything but stare. I felt terrible about not telling him the whole truth, but it was better he should think I'd had some deep wounds I'd recovered from than know I was a flighty serial dater.

I certainly didn't want to discuss my romantic adventures with him. Not Filipe in Venice or Tomas in Oslo, or the whole episode in Rome with the Scottish soccer player whose name escaped me. Suffice it to say, once I grew into myself, I managed to have some fun in my life. I just hadn't met Mr. Right yet. All of which wasn't something Devon needed to know.

"Listen, I have to head back over to Matilda's. Will you be all right by yourself?" Devon looked as if he wanted to stay but needed to go.

"Of course. I have 99, so I'm not by myself." Actually, I was relieved to have Devon go. I needed a little space to sort through my feelings where he was concerned. I'd begun to like having him around. Maybe too much.

CHAPTER THIRTEEN

THE NEXT MORNING, I RECEIVED A TEXT JUST AFTER I'D WOKEN WITH the oddest tickling on my face and a significant weight on my chest—and very loud purring.

Devon: Gotta run, new assignment. Keep me posted on the boxes.

His short message without a sorry, a talk to you soon, or even a goodbye was exactly why I didn't do local. Not that Devon was a local anymore or that we'd done anything. So why did I feel a bone-deep disappointment?

I contacted my mom about the text and found out Devon was off on another adventure, and we were all left to our own devices. It seemed more than a bit odd he would just take off that way. I didn't like it, especially under the circumstances, but I was sure he wouldn't leave me alone if he thought I was in any real danger. Whoever had sent the postcard was undoubtedly the person who had broken into my house, but with the new security system Devon had installed, I at least felt relatively safe.

My mom also told me a new shipment had come into the store, and I needed to photograph it all and get it uploaded to the website. That was great news because the shipment meant I had something to keep my mind off stalkers and blackmailers —who very well might be the same person or persons. In addition, keeping busy meant I wouldn't have to worry about keeping secrets from Devon. Out of sight, out of mind, as they say. Or was it absence makes the heart grow fonder?

After giving 99 a complete set of instructions—including not climbing on top of the cupboards and hiding—I headed over to the store, hoping for a little normality while keeping an eye out for any strangers.

When I got to the store, everything waited in the back room for me. Though the items were impressive, it was a huge haul. My mom did like to buy on a hunch, but I was shocked at how much stuff there was.

"Come look at these," I said as she floated by, seemingly on cloud nine from the influx of treasures.

Two Tiffany lamps sat next to a copper Buddha. A Scandinavian butter box rested next to a vintage tin diner sign. Not the usual assortment, though there must have been a reason behind each eclectic piece.

"Oh, Pippa," she said with delight in her voice. "You found the Buddha. How wonderful."

"Yes, but this is an unusual collection. I agree the items are fabulous, but why did you buy so much? Seems a bit impulsive, even for you."

"Oh, a few weeks ago, I received an email from an auction house stating that a wealthy yet somewhat eccentric woman up in San Francisco had passed away, and they were auctioning her estate online. The estate was divided into two lots, but with great restraint, I only bid on one. I promise we'll get rid of anything we don't want."

Famous last words. I shook my head and decided I'd need to go online that night and research the woman who'd owned all this. Understanding the history behind the items would help me write better copy for the website. Doing so might also help me figure if my mother was keeping another of her secrets—because I had a feeling her curious purchase wasn't quite as simple as she tried to make out.

When I got home, the house was eerily quiet, even with 99 greeting me at the door, so I welcomed the chance to dive into some research to occupy my mind. I found what I needed very quickly. When someone wealthy died, regardless of how empty their life might have been, there was a story.

I read the first few pieces I came across and got a sense that the woman, Nadia McConnell, was, in fact, a fascinating person. Her grandfather was the renowned explorer Winston McConnell, who captained a ship that went down in the South Atlantic off the coast of Brazil. Nadia's grandmother, Beatrice, inherited millions and became a philanthropist, focusing on saving the rainforest. Nadia's father, Winston II, studied history and traveled the world, searching for ancient treasures, many of which Nadia still had. I wondered if our little haul contained any of those items. I would have to check more thoroughly. There was no mention of Nadia's mother anywhere or any surviving relatives, which was odd. Most obituaries featured both parents. Another mystery. Seemed to be the story of my life lately.

I returned to the store the next day, photographed some more of the pieces, then continued my research. I started following all the little links buried in each article. My new laptop, which I'd named Roadrunner after the swift-running chaparral bird, was way faster than my old one. The more I clicked, the more I discovered. When my dad found me hours later, I was cross-legged on the floor, Roadrunner in my lap, still clicking away.

"Pip, time to close up," he said somewhat hesitantly. He

knew when I was in the zone not to startle me. "Your mother would like you to join us for supper if you don't have any plans." Dad knew perfectly well I had no plans. With Devon gone, I was back to my old life, which admittedly seemed just a bit emptier.

"Sure, Dad, if you're cooking!" I grinned up at him. We knew my mom had many talents, none of which were culinary in nature. Regardless, I'd hoped to spend some time with my dad. I was curious about how much he knew about the money. I assumed he knew at least a bit. Had he thought she'd won the lottery? On second thought, maybe I needed to question my mom. I wanted to know why I couldn't say anything to Devon—not just about the money, but about the blackmailing, which was the most worrying. The more I considered it, the more I was convinced something else was going on. Either way, I had to uncover the truth. I couldn't just sit on the sidelines.

My mother, however, was a master evader and managed to avoid all my questions that night and the next two nights. Nevertheless, I'd made it a habit of dining with them that week, so on Thursday, I tried again.

"Mom, Devon said he lives in Virginia now."

"He told you that?"

Now, why would she be surprised? "Of course, why wouldn't he?"

"Oh, no reason at all. What else did he tell you?"

Right then, I knew she was hiding something about Devon. I wasn't sure if I could fool her into thinking I knew what she knew. My deceptive skills were not that good, though I was certainly working on them. In the end, I changed the subject.

"Tell me more about this estate you bought. Who was Nadia McConnell?" Mom didn't know I'd looked Nadia up.

"Oh, she was a wealthy heiress, as I said. She was a spinster with no apparent heirs. Speaking of spinsters, how are things progressing for you?"

"What? Are you saying I'm a spinster?"

"Don't be silly, but you and Devon have been spending quite a bit of time together. I mean, he's practically living with you."

"It was two nights, and one of those was in a... Never mind." I wasn't going to tell my mom anything more about Devon. If she wouldn't reveal anything, then neither would I.

My dad put down his fork. "Kate, leave Pip alone. She and Devon will take things at their own pace."

That was the last straw. Even my dad tried to play Cupid. If I thought there was anything between Devon and me, I still wouldn't have told them, but I'd not heard anything from Devon since he'd left. His silence had made it obvious I'd got our dynamics wrong.

With a sigh, I realized I wouldn't learn anything from my mom. I considered asking Prudence what she knew, as my mom told her everything, but Prudence would just call my mother and blab. I'd already tried to talk to Babs to see if she'd found anything more about the blackmailing, but she didn't have a clue and oddly didn't seem to want to know, which was maybe not so odd. All these revelations had threatened her bland, staid existence, and she just couldn't deal. When it came to the Vegas caper, and every other secret in Luckland, it was up to me.

By Friday, I was more than ready to kick back in my own house, maybe binge-watch all eight hours of the original BBC *Pride and Prejudice*, or if the urge struck, work on my blog... Until my doorbell buzzed, paired with a rattling of the doorknob. I didn't have a lot of visitors. Aside from family and a few friends, nobody stopped by except the water meter reader. So, after the postcard, the break-in, and those times I'd felt someone watching me, no way in hell would I just open the door. At least not without peering through the window first. What if there was some guy in a hockey mask on my porch?

I took one look and flung open the door.

"Dani!" I practically screeched.

"Pippiiiii!"

We did our secret greeting dance we'd made up at the ripe old age of six or so. Two steps to the right. Two steps to the left. Shimmy down and shimmy up, and a great big hug to top it off. God, I'd missed her.

"When did you get back? Why didn't you tell me you were coming? Come in, hurry! I've got so much to tell you. You won't believe what's been going on!" I grabbed her arm and pulled her inside.

She laughed as she dropped her bags in the front hall. Dani always stayed with me when she was back in town. Her parents had retired a few years ago and moved to Tucson, and naturally, my home became Dani's home. I introduced her to 99, and Dani, being a cat lover, immediately scooped her up for some serious cuddles. We then headed into the kitchen. She grabbed the wine, I grabbed the glasses, and we headed out to my back porch. She'd been gone for over two months, so there was a ton to catch up on.

"Before I tell you all that's been happening, tell me about your adventure. I mean, the South Pacific had to be spectacular, right? Bali? Tahiti? Bora Bora? You could have called occasionally."

"Yeah, but you saw every Instagram post, so you know where I was at all times." She grinned. True, I did know, but I just liked to hear about her trips as she was a wonderful storyteller. In high school, we thought we'd travel the world and write coffee table books.

"I did, and it must have been marvelous because you look fantastic." Dani always looked fantastic, but she got even more beautiful when in the tropical sun. It was all in the genes. Her father was from the Dominican Republic and played pro ball. Her mother was from Cuba. Dani had that honey-colored, flawless skin, fabulously thick wavy hair that always seemed to just fall into place, and a smile that absolutely dazzled. We met in kindergarten. First day. We lined up to go out for recess, grabbed the other's hand, and never let go. Everyone deserved a friend like that.

"It was amazing. I'll give you that." She smiled. "Nothing like being paid to do what you love and see the world all at the same time."

I was admittedly jealous. I'd thought about learning to dive and exploring underwater photography, but while I loved to travel, I also enjoyed being comfortable. If I was going out on a chartered yacht in the South Pacific, I wanted to remain above deck. I wasn't cut out for crew quarters. My dream job was photographing the alps, with my base camp being a château on Lake Lucerne.

"What's been happening here, Pip? I got a text from your sister saying that all hell had broken loose."

"You didn't come back because of a hysterical text from Babs, did you?" If so, I would personally strangle her.

"Ha! As if, but I am interested in knowing what kind of hell she was talking about."

I wondered if the promise my mom extracted from me about not telling a soul included Dani. No. I had to tell her. Never in my life had I kept a secret from her, and I wasn't about to start now. Besides, how could I tell her about the postcard and the break-in while leaving out the rest? I couldn't—it would be impossible.

Plunging in, I started with the yard sale, the boxes, and Devon's arrival back in Luckland. I didn't want to leave out a single detail, but it took a while with all her interruptions. Dani was like that. She especially liked the part where Devon showed up.

"Doesn't sound like the Devon I remember. What is he like now?"

"Indiana Jones meets James Bond," I said with no hesitation.

Dani grinned. "You better get him back here so I can verify. I would have thought he'd have turned out to be more of the nutty professor type. I can't believe you didn't jump his bones. Are you nuts?"

"This is Devon we're talking about, so my usual short-term fling would not be appropriate."

"Okay... I get it, but what a damn shame." She laughed. "Now, tell me more about the money. It's not in the boxes, is it?"

"No. I'm not sure what's in the boxes other than some details on where they spent the money, but that brings me to the postcard." Knowing how she'd react, I told her about the written threat, the break-in, and the feeling someone had been watching me, which, as predicted, brought out the Amazon warrior within her.

"How did you not tell me this was happening? I would have come back here in a flash. Do we need a security detail? I've got a few navy SEALs at my beck and call."

"Devon's got it covered. At least, I think so. He's wired up the house like Fort Knox."

"So, someone is stalking you, the posse have millions in stolen loot, and Devon, Matilda's *son* Devon, is here to rescue you all but can't know what's happening? Not buying it. Something else is going on, and I bet Devon is part of it."

"I don't know, Dani. I do know the women seem to think Devon has something to do with me, especially after the Tarot reading."

"The what?"

With a sigh, I told her all about the cards and Marcy's statement that they revealed something about my love life. "Before she could explain, the lot of them scattered, but it's not as if I believe in all that stuff anyway."

Dani burst out laughing—so hard it seemed her stomach spasmed. She almost fell off her chair.

"Why is any of this funny?" I asked her, a little miffed.

"I can't believe you don't remember," she managed to say between gasping for breaths, still holding her stomach.

"Clearly, I don't, so remind me."

"Remember when we went to the fair? We were fourteen, I think, and we went to the gypsy tent? She had that crystal ball, and we sat there while she told us our future?"

I searched my memory. Eventually, a picture emerged, and I remembered an oldish woman with a fake accent and a wig. "She said the next young man I saw was my future," I remarked somewhat dryly. "Then we walked out and ran right into Devon. You hounded me for weeks after that. It wasn't funny. Or true. She was just a carnival worker."

"Yeah, but Marcy isn't, and those cards may well say Devon is your one true love." Dani continued laughing, and I almost threw something at her.

"What cards did she draw? Tell me," she demanded.

Luckily, I remembered. "Three cards. The first was the Eight of Swords. The middle card was The Star. The third card was the Ace of Cups."

While I talked, Dani frantically typed into her phone. I waited for her to scan through whatever she'd found.

"So, there's a site that lets you input your layout and get an interpretation."

"And?" I waited, holding my breath.

"Well, it's based on the position of each card. So, in this case, it says that first card, the Eight of Swords, is your past influencing you by keeping you from moving forward. You're afraid of something. The Star tells you to be optimistic and offers you hope for a new beginning. The Ace of Cups... Well, that's a doozy, Pip."

"Come on, Dani, spill it."

"It signifies love and happiness for your new relationship. Looks as if Devon's the one, Pip."

I took a moment to digest it all, then after a moment, when I decided I wasn't sure whether to believe what Dani had told me, I shrugged. "Come on, let's go inside."

We grabbed some blankets and pillows and opted for a sleepover in the living room with 99 joining us. It was the kind of sleepover we had growing up. Stay up, gab, and watch a movie. It was exactly what I needed. I poured us another glass of wine, but then Dani sighed.

"So good news, bad news, girl," she said, suddenly contemplative. "I'm only in town for the weekend. Then I'm off again."

"Where's the good news in that?"

"It's another charter, but this one is off the Florida coast. At least I'll be a bit closer to home this time."

Though used to her comings and goings, I missed having her around. I missed having a friend I could confide in, bounce ideas off, and spend time with regularly. Mom said, in those moments when we managed to have a conversation of any significance, that if I would just find someone and settle down, I too could have that. I told her to find me a male version of Dani with a matching personality. Then we'd talk.

CHAPTER FOURTEEN

On Saturday, Dani and I headed up to the Mile High City for some fun. After we booked a room at a trendy downtown hotel in the heart of everything, we went to a ball game, then dinner at a highly rated gastro pub, followed by a little clubbing. Always a little clubbing when we were in Denver.

We were on our third venue when we met a couple of guys worth more than five minutes of our time. We had a few drinks with them and some fairly lively conversation—if there was such a thing in a dance club. Then we hit the dance floor. Realistically, Dani and I were probably just dancing with ourselves more so than with Paul and Jim, or was it Peter and Tim?

Then my phone buzzed.

Devon: Hey, Red.

If I were the suspicious sort, I'd question his timing. After not hearing from him for nearly a week, why had he contacted me in the middle of a full-on girl's night out? I considered ignoring him, but I just couldn't. It wasn't my style. So, instead of having fun, I focused on coming up with some wit to throw back at him. I was still contemplating what to say when Dani came over to the table I'd managed to snag. She stood over me, her hands on her hips.

"What are you doing? Put that away."

"I got a text from Devon. I have to respond, and I have to be clever."

She grabbed the phone, and after a few quick taps of her thumbs, handed it back. It seemed she'd done the honors for me.

Me: Hey.

"Dani, that's not clever. His text clearly required something more."

"And you are clearly wasting an opportunity. Leave it to Devon. His timing is impeccable, isn't it?" she asked as our eyes met. She was right. It couldn't be a coincidence. It was as if he had eyes on me. I glanced at my phone and wondered which app he'd installed was the culprit. When my phone buzzed again, Dani grabbed it before I could even look. Smirking, she handed it back. Devon had sent an emoji—the one with the sunglasses. I knew I should have gone with an emoji, and now he'd beaten me to it. At that precise moment, I realized Devon had wormed his way under my skin and taken my heart. Dani knew it too.

"Come on, let's head out. None of the guys here are interesting anyway."

Truthfully, we wouldn't have gone anywhere with anyone we'd just met in a bar, but thanks to Devon, I wasn't even tempted. Well damn.

Monday came too fast for me, and with it, my goodbyes to Dani, but I felt totally rejuvenated after a weekend in her company. Not because I could unload on her, but I also got to catch up on all her latest news, like the fact she'd met someone on her last diving expedition, and it looked as if he might have the makings for a long-term relationship. Hard to say with Dani, but she didn't seem to be speaking of him in the past tense as she usually did when she'd decided to cut her ties. In fact, if things went well, there was a chance I'd get to meet him. She even hinted she might bring him next time. We'd see. I was in a reasonably good mood heading into the shop, which naturally brought the *inquisitor* over.

"Good morning, Pippa. Aren't you in a chipper mood!"

"Good morning, Mom, and yes, I'm in a fine mood. Thanks for noticing." Though I still wasn't happy about someone breaking into my house and blackmailing the ladies, all in all, I did feel better. I'd also devised a plan to get my dad talking, and the idea was clever if I did say so myself. So, I waited for just the right moment and caught him between projects at the front of the store.

"Hey, Dad. I'm curious. What was the first piece you guys bought for the shop?"

"Hmmm. Technically, we bought the shop itself from Mr. Frost way back when. He'd put the whole business up for sale. Lock, stock, and barrel, as they say. He never cleared out the inventory. It came with the place."

"Oh, that's right, I'd forgotten! That must have been awfully expensive. Where did you come up with that kind of capital?"

"Capital?"

"Yes. I only ask because I've been thinking about opening a studio. I'm researching the costs, but I have no idea how I'm going to make it happen." I wanted to see him field that one!

"Pippa, I thought your mother had that discussion with you. Uncle Ernie left her a tidy little sum."

I couldn't believe he'd brought up Uncle Ernie. Did he really think we *had* an Uncle Ernie? Though admittedly, just over a week ago, I did too. Damn.

"Why don't you talk to her about funding your studio? I'm sure there's enough to get you started."

Though the studio was a cover story, the idea was starting to gel. I could have a studio. Money could do that. "Thanks, Dad, that's a good idea. I just need to find the right time, I think." Realistically, talking to my mom about money and blackmail at the moment was probably a horrible idea—almost as bad as Babs's yard sale. The studio, however, was a great idea. Once all the nerve-racking hubbub was over, I would create a plan. Or try to. Though never much of a planner, I could learn.

I spent the rest of the day taking photos and getting some actual work done. Life was back to normal, almost. The images on my Meadow Bloom post were stunning, and I'd finally sat down and finished writing the article, which I was just about ready to upload. Writing about something meant to be experienced in person was a challenge for any blogger. The vision was about taking the reader there through imagery and prose. Taking someone on a virtual tour of Mongolia would be a heck of a lot easier than a blooming meadow in the Rockies, but I let the photos speak for themselves and hoped they would do the trick.

About to take off for the day, I paused when the storefront chimes jangled, and in walked Luckland's newest residents. Having not officially met them, I had no idea what I was supposed to say when meeting someone dressed in pinstripe suits, matching bowler hats, wingtip shoes, and canes with gargoyles on the handle. They may have been going for distinguished. However, their ensemble all added up to a classic fail. I wasn't even sure why they'd dressed alike. They certainly didn't look alike. One was tall, bald, and lanky, and the other short, stocky, and with a mullet. Both were about my dad's age, which was early sixties, and they had the most horrific orange tans—not the tanning bed kind, the tanning bottle kind, with white circles around their eyes.

The tall one held out a hand. "Pleased to meet you," he said, in a bizarre, affected way. I couldn't quite place the accent.

"You too," I replied while trying to shake off the odd sensation riding my spine.

The short man held out his hand as well. "Good afternoon, madam," he said, though his voice was quite different—deeper and gravelly.

As they didn't tell me their names, I didn't tell them mine. "Can I help you with something?"

"Is the lady of the establishment here?" the tall man asked in his peculiar voice. I waited for him to crack a smile as it was such a strange question, but he remained stone-faced.

"I'm sorry, she's left for the day. Perhaps the gentleman of the house could assist?" I smiled politely, but I must have offended them.

They simply thanked me, turned right around, and marched out in unison. I quickly locked the front door so they couldn't change their minds and come back in. After a moment, I called out to my dad that I was leaving, then headed out to my Jeep. Unfortunately, not only had the unusual men creeped me out, but I was also back to the impression someone was watching me. I raced to my car, then drove home as fast as the speed limit allowed. In moments like those, I wished Devon had stuck around.

The second I entered my home to find everything as I'd left it, I relaxed, but that was when my phone buzzed.

Devon: Tomorrow. 7 a.m. Trailhead.

Me: 8. I don't do 7.

Though pleased about being all snappy, I couldn't believe

Devon was back. I also didn't understand why he couldn't have simply called me. I really wouldn't have minded hearing that sexy baritone of his. Better yet, he could have knocked on my door. I might have let him in. Definitely might have.

Devon: 7:30, then.

Me: Fine. But you better bring coffee.

If there was one thing I'd learned in my life, it was never to let a man get too bossy, or they'd steamroll right over you. I had no idea what game Devon and I were playing, but even with my nerves back on edge, I was kind of looking forward to it.

CHAPTER FIFTEEN

I didn't sleep that night. Not a wink nor a smidge. First, I stared at the ceiling, listening to the wind whip around the house's eaves, but every time a tree branch snapped, I jumped. Then I tried to think about something pleasant—like Devon. Although, thinking about Devon just made me wonder what was happening with us and why we were meeting in the morning. I'd thought about bringing my camera and getting some more shots in, but what if our meeting was of the clandestine shoebox variety or something else entirely?

If he wanted to talk about the goings-on with the Luckland posse, I doubted whether I could keep from telling him about the blackmail or what was in the boxes. I was still looking for a good reason not to tell him because keeping quiet weighed on me big time, which was why I couldn't sleep. Morning could not come soon enough. Even 99 was fed up with me tossing and turning.

Sometime during the night, I realized I couldn't meet Devon looking as I usually did. I needed to show up to his little rendezvous looking so hot he would swallow his tongue. I also realized the Tarot reading had begun to influence my behavior in a teeny tiny way. So, at the crack of dawn, I dived out of bed.

Transforming into a siren for Devon's benefit was not a simple task when I had to dress for a hike. It would have been way easier if I could have thrown on my little black dress. Making myself look smoking hot in jeans and hiking boots took enormous attention to detail, but I was definitely up for the challenge.

I chose jeans that fit like a glove, and a snug tank under a loose cotton blouse. Next, I did something I rarely did; I left my hair down. It was relatively long and full of curls, so I almost always kept it braided. Still, for magnetic qualities, I had to leave it down. 99 watched me while I took a quick selfie and sent it to Dani—not that I needed confirmation my look was perfect, but a second opinion wouldn't hurt. Not long after, I got a tick of approval from Dani, so I headed out.

The plan was to meet Devon at the trailhead, take my coffee, have a chat, stun him with my charm and beauty, and head over to the shop. However, when I got to the trailhead, there was no sign of him. His rental car was there. Just not Devon. Frustrated, I texted him.

Me: Where are you? I'm in the parking lot.
Devon: Headed to the meadow.
Me: Just stop and wait. Are we clear?
Devon: Clear as mud, Red.

So much for wearing my hair down and making an entrance. I'd have to settle with being me with hair sticking to the back of my neck. The sun wasn't intense yet, and thankfully I always carried one of my hats. I had an entire collection. Every place I'd been, I picked up a hat, from ball caps to sombreros to berets. I grabbed a basic Rockies visor. Not the best headgear for my "meeting" with Devon, but it would do.

Devon hadn't gotten much of a head start as he was only

about a half-mile up the trail. Had I known, I would have made him turn around and come back.

"Why didn't you wait, Flash?" I asked as I approached.

"Hello to you too, Red." He grinned as he handed my coffee over. At least he hadn't forgotten that.

"Okay, spill it. Why are we here?" I took a few good sips of coffee, which had the precise amount of cream. Damn him. Then he handed me a scone and pointed to a small blanket he'd laid out in the grass along the side of the trail. I was so stupidly charmed I didn't even care he hadn't answered me. I sat down, put my coffee and scone on the blanket, then did what any other woman would do—I removed my hat and shook out my hair.

His poleaxed expression was priceless and exactly what I'd intended. I was officially every girl in a Bruno Mars song. Devon hadn't seen me with my hair down since, well, maybe never.

"Now, Devon, would you like to share with me what this is about?" I smiled and looked directly at him. Not easy because his eyes were killer. They flashed blue and green with sparkly little flecks of gold. I waited. Then waited some more until, finally, he seemed to recover.

"Boxes."

I frowned. "Boxes?"

"Yeah, I have a lead on the boxes," he said.

"And?"

"I don't believe I've ever seen you with your hair down like that."

He leaned over and brushed a few wayward strands out of my eyes. Well damn. My heart raced, and I wondered fleetingly if my face appeared flushed and if he sensed my reaction. Slowly, he started to lean in, and I was sure I parted my lips...

The loud chatter of a group of birdwatchers pulled Devon

and me apart. Binoculars and safari hats could kill a perfect moment. Spell broken.

I grinned. "Where were we?"

"Boxes." He grinned back, though his was a bit wicked. "I think I may have a lead on who has them, but I need you to keep this to yourself. Don't say anything to anyone, especially the Vegas Divas."

Okay, that was funny, but the secrecy thing needed to stop. I wasn't cut out for it. So, instead of agreeing, I asked what I thought was a reasonable question. "Who is your suspect?"

"The Panello brothers. Luckland's newest residents. Have you met them yet?"

"Oh, yes, but I didn't know their names. You think they have the boxes?"

"They're the most likely. They frequent yard sales, including yours, sorry, your sister's. They're also strangers in town, and we know the locals would have returned Kate's dead relatives."

"That's your lead? That's not new information," I said, disappointed.

"Fair enough, but what if I told you they didn't arrive from Seychelles, as rumored, but arrived from Las Vegas."

Vegas, as depicted on the postcard, on which someone had threatened me just before they broke into my house. "Could be a coincidence, but you're right. It does sound suspicious. Is there more?" I hoped so because knowing those two creepy guys might be my stalkers was not a comforting thought.

"One of the kids helping at the yard sale saw the Panellos carrying four of the boxes to their car." He gave a smug smile. "And there was a security camera above the garage door right where they'd parked."

"That's not a lead, Devon. That's crucial evidence!" It was suddenly crystal clear the Panellos were involved in everything going on. However, Devon didn't know the half of it. He must have read something in my expression because he frowned and eyed me so suspiciously, I wanted to hide.

"What? Spill it."

It took some effort to hold his gaze while knowing I also had important information that could help sort out the mess the ladies had gotten themselves into. If the Panellos had the boxes, it seemed kind of obvious they were the ones blackmailing the ladies, and Devon needed to know. "Can you promise me this won't go further?"

"Promise," he said, holding up three fingers in the Boy Scout salute. "On my honor."

I almost smiled, but what I had to tell him wasn't funny. I took a deep breath. "You know when you asked me what prompted the ladies to tell Babs and me about the money?"

Devon nodded.

"Well, it's because someone is blackmailing them. They received phone calls during a book club meeting. The caller said they knew the women's secrets."

"Secrets? More secrets, or is it to do with the money?"

"Um, Pru said 'everything else,' but no one would tell me what."

"But the secrets were in the shoeboxes, and now they think whoever has the boxes is trying to blackmail them? Did the person who called ask for money or something else?"

"I don't think so. The ladies didn't say."

Devon lifted an eyebrow. "Did they say anything else?"

I didn't want to divulge more confidences, but I'd already told him most of them. "The paperwork that revealed what they'd done with the Vegas money was in the shoeboxes. Though I don't think that's part of the 'secrets' they're really worried about." From the ladies' reaction, the paper trail seemed to be the least of their concerns. Something in those boxes was far more vital to them. "So, what do we do now? We really need to get those boxes back."

Devon sighed. "Yes, we do, and I have an idea. I need you to see if we can get into the Panellos' house."

"You want to break into their house? Are you nuts? Isn't that a bit extreme?" I liked a good adventure as well as the next person, but that was entering new territory. My response earned me one of his *don't be ridiculous* looks.

"No, just get them to buy something they can't take home themselves, and we'll deliver it. It shouldn't be too difficult. Flash those emerald green eyes and a smile or two, and I'm betting they'll buy the whole store."

He went on to explain his plan, but I didn't pay enough attention. Flattery would do that to me. I gathered we'd deliver some piece of furniture, and while I chatted away, he would look around. Or something like that. I agreed to the whole thing without thinking it through because lately, Devon seemed to scramble my brain. I actually hesitated when he stood and held out his hand to help me up, afraid if I touched him, the sparks would set off a brush fire. I got to my feet on my own, and by Devon's smirk, he knew why.

We didn't say anything more as we headed to the parking lot. Devon seemed deep in thought, and I simply watched him, happier than I'd felt for a long time. It was as if sunshine had broken through clouds when all I'd expected was rain.

As soon as I got into my Jeep, Devon gave me a lopsided grin. "See ya, Red." Then he sauntered toward his car

As I drove away, I realized I had no idea when I'd see him again, but I couldn't wait until I did.

CHAPTER SIXTEEN

I arrived at the store just in time to see Babs also pulling in. She usually popped in a few times a week with my niece Leah in tow so my parents could have some quality time with their granddaughter. I could have used a little toddler relief right about then, so I happily took her by the hand as we headed to the shop. When we reached the back patio with a pair of wicker chairs, a cute little tile-topped table, and a few potted plants, Babs gently took my arm.

"Pip, I have news. Very, very exciting news. Mother and Father will be over the moon to hear it, so I'll tell you all when we get inside."

Considering Babs's great exaggerating skills and her participation in recent disasters, I wasn't holding my breath *I'd* be over the moon.

"Mother, Father, it's Babs," she called as soon as the door shut behind us.

"We're here," Leah said, mimicking Babs's tone.

Our parents hurried from the front of the store with big smiles. "We didn't expect you, dear. What a pleasant surprise!" Mom said.

"No, Grammy, Mommy has a surprise for you!" Leah squealed.

"Oh, she does? Well then, let's all sit and perhaps take a calming breath." My mom seemed to notice the way Babs practically bopped up and down with excitement.

We all gathered around a brand-new arrival—a six-foot circular table, circa 1920 or so, badly in need of restoration. My dad grabbed some bridge chairs he stored in the back, and we waited as Babs situated herself for her grand presentation.

"Without further ado, I am excited to announce..."

Babs looked at Leah, who tapped her hands on the table and yelled, "Drumroll, please." My dad and I laughed. It was always easy to laugh with Leah around.

Babs smiled. "I have a new career, and I wanted you all to be the first to know. I am officially a working woman." The silence was palpable. My mother's shocked expression captured my feelings exactly. Babs's news was truly the last thing we ever expected to come out of her mouth.

"Do tell," I said with just a bit of skepticism. I couldn't imagine Babs going to work; she was simply not the type.

"The Panellos have employed me to redecorate their lovely new home. Isn't that exciting? You see, they came over to the house yesterday to meet with Tom about some structural something or other and noticed how lovely our home was. Naturally, they asked who my decorator was. When I said I did the decorating myself, they immediately offered me the job of bringing their home up to snuff."

Babs had just thrown a monkey wrench into the plan Devon and I had made to recover the boxes. Actually, that monkey wrench was more like a wrecking ball. Trust Babs to create the latest disaster, albeit unintentionally. I couldn't blame her for not wanting to pass up such a super opportunity. She had great decorating skills, and it would be a good career choice, but Babs had no clue about the Panellos, who were simply not the right clients. In reality, they were possibly the very *worst* clients. If Devon's suspicions were correct, the Panellos could genuinely have bad intentions toward my mother and her friends, and I wasn't allowed to tell anyone. Damn Devon for making me promise not to say anything!

"This calls for a celebration," my dad said as he got up to give Babs a hug.

"Agreed, my house, seven-thirty tonight. Don't bring a thing." My mother was all smiles. I was in full-blown panic mode, so I checked my phone and acted surprised.

"Wow, would you look at the time? I'd love to chat about this, but I've gotta run, photo emergency."

As soon as I got outside, I debated whether to text Devon and give him the news. If he was going to my mom's, I could tell him then, but I didn't know if he'd be there. I didn't even know if he was in Luckland or not.

I headed home and waited until mid-afternoon before deciding he needed forewarning. I considered calling him, but as he seemed to prefer texts more, I went ahead and fired off the alert.

Me: Houston, we have a problem.

Devon: 10-4. See you tonight, Red.

So, he knew. He must officially be in town. Typical, how I was always the last to know. Secrets and lies—Luckland style.

I needed to relax before my mom's shindig, and the best way was to take a long, soaking bath. My hiking attire worked that morning, but for the celebration, I figured I'd go all out and slip into my little black dress, which I'd hung on the back of the door to steam out the wrinkles. As any girl knew, the little black dress was a marvelous tool; it worked on any shape or size and always brought out the best in whoever wore it. Thing was, as a photographer, I had one basic tenet. All the preening and prep in the world couldn't make anyone beautiful; it could only reveal what was already on the inside. I was making all that effort simply to ensure Devon recognized he was in the presence of utter awesomeness—namely, me. I also had to make sure he was there before me and arrive a little late to make a grand entrance.

That night was supposed to be all about my sister, and it would be. I was just going to steal a minute of glory, which I knew she'd support. In my awkward high school years, I'd once daydreamed about being someone's someone, someday—and though I never expected that someone to be Devon, that day had come.

Nervous, I pulled up to my mom's house and spotted Devon's sedan. So, my timing was perfect. Once I'd parked, I carefully walked around to the back, as heels and gravel didn't mix well, and headed up the few steps to the sprawling patio. In the far corner, I spotted my dad manning the grill, with Devon apparently serving as sous chef. I paused for just a moment, silently willing them to turn their heads my way. Well, Devon, anyway. When he did, it was another triumphant moment for me, though the way our eyes locked, he might have considered it his moment as well. He, too, looked awfully snazzy. There was something about a guy in a white cotton dress shirt with the sleeves rolled up. The shirt most definitely emphasized his broad shoulders, flat stomach, slim waist... Good lord, I was a goner.

"Nailed it, Sis," Babs said beside me. I grinned as I turned to her.

"Thanks. Congratulations on your job, by the way. I'm sorry I didn't say it before." I was still terrified Devon's plan would fall apart because of her, but she deserved the praise. I glanced around to see where the infamous Panello brothers were and found them over at the side table, chatting with my mom.

Good. I just had to stay relaxed. I'd gotten surprisingly good at all the undercover spy stuff. I'd even brought my camera, but I'd left it in the car so as not to diminish my grand entrance. Deciding now was a good time to retrieve it, I proceeded through the house.

"Leaving so soon, Red?"

I practically jumped fifteen feet in the air. "You know that took years off my life, Magnum. And no, just going to get my camera."

"I'll join you."

That wasn't in my plan. I'd planned to get the camera and, while out there, call Dani. After the win of capturing Devon's attention, I needed some BFF time.

"Fine." I walked straight out the front door and down the steps to the driveway without stopping. He kept pace, not saying a word. When we got to the car, I grabbed my stuff and headed back. Devon stayed right along next to me.

"Devon, is there something you wanted?"

"Nope, just making sure you're safe. That's all."

"We're at my mom's house."

"I'm aware, though you might want to consider the guest list?"

God, I hated when he was right. The Panello brothers struck again. I sighed but was glad Devon was there to protect me.

"How's 99?" he asked.

"She misses you." I glanced at him because I was talking about myself.

"Does she?" He grinned because he knew what I meant. "So, how'd you like to help me out tonight? I have a plan."

"I'm all in, Kemosabe." I had no idea what the plan was, but it couldn't be too dangerous.

"I want you to be on the lookout for empty glasses from the

Panellos. When you spot them, carefully put them aside, don't wash them."

"Dev, I'm not questioning your methods, but if we already know they have the boxes, why do we need their fingerprints? I assume that's why you want me to collect their glasses."

"Yes, but we'll talk about it later. Just see if you can snatch those for us."

By then, we were out on the patio, where things were in full swing. Sitting at the infamous round table were the Vegas Divas —as Devon called them—along with Babs, and the Panello brothers in their latest outfits. Leisure suits. They wore seventies velour leisure suits. I schooled my face and approached with caution.

"Pippa, dear, have you met Freddie and Frankie Panello?" Prudence asked with a lavish smile.

"We have met but not properly introduced," I said as I took a seat. I pretended to listen to their chatter, but their voices were just too annoying. Instead, I tried to zero in on Devon's conversation with my dad over at the grill. I kept my eye on the brothers' glasses though, and when they were just about empty, I offered them a refill, which they accepted.

Without further ado, I took the glasses into the kitchen, looked around to make sure no one watched me, then continued out to my Jeep, where I placed the glasses in a spare reusable grocery bag. Feeling triumphant at accomplishing my mission, I grabbed a tripod out of the back as I didn't want my trip to the car to appear suspicious. I set up the tripod in the backyard, then stopped at the drinks table to pour the brothers a new glass of red wine. All seemed well until I heard Prudence in the middle of the worst story she could have chosen. She was literally telling them about the bachelorette party in Vegas. Thankfully, she'd just gotten to Matilda and the lounge singer, but I needed to shut her up, so I did the first thing that popped into my head—I tripped and spilled the wine on Prudence. She shrieked, which brought Devon running with my dad close behind. The disco duo hurriedly grabbed whatever napkins they could find and began patting her down. I suspected she enjoyed that. My mother, however, did what any mother would do.

"Really, Pippa," she said quite loudly. For once, I didn't care. I needed to cause a ruckus and disrupt the story. It wasn't as if Prudence was going to tell them about the money but telling them about the trip to Vegas if these two guys were involved in the casino heist was asking for trouble. Babs looked furious, and I couldn't blame her. It must have seemed as if I were purposely ruining her night. In contrast, Matilda looked ready to burst into laughter. Hope, of course, had turned to Marcy and was comparing the current fiasco to a movie she once saw. I apologized to Prudence, then slipped away to escape everyone's scrutiny.

"Quite a show, Red. Well done." Devon's whisper and the light touch he placed on the small of my back sent goose bumps over my skin, but before I could say anything, he returned to the crowded table where the subject now focused on the best solutions for red wine stains.

I bit my lip to hide a smile. I'd take his approval for a win. My second that night. I was on a roll.

Mom served dinner shortly after. I snagged a seat next to my dad, off in the corner. Everyone else had crammed themselves around the giant table, all talking at once. I still wondered if my dad was bluffing about Uncle Ernie. For a second, I thought about asking Dad about the money one more time, but he seemed so relaxed. We also had the wild and crazy strangers among us, so I decided to leave the conversation for another day. Besides, I heard Marcy and Hope discussing the mob of people they'd been serving all week at the café. It seemed every day was packed with new faces, and curiously, almost everyone ordered lasagna.

"You know how tourists are," my mom said. "They find that little favorite place and tell everyone they know about it."

The people gathered around the table nodded, seemingly in agreement.

"We've had a huge jump in store traffic as well. Even though we are nowhere near Founders' Day, Pippa may have nailed it on that gold-hunting thing."

"Well, whatever it is, it's good for business, and it's good for Luckland," Matilda said.

I wasn't so sure. As a newly anointed crime victim, I would have preferred they all just stayed away for a bit.

CHAPTER SEVENTEEN

I stuck around after everyone cleared out to help my mom clear up. Babs, who had now entered the twentieth century, being a working woman and all, bailed early. I didn't mind—quiet time with my mom was a valuable commodity. A conversation was also in order. All this secret stuff was too much. With my mom and the ladies on one side, and Devon on the other, they were pulling me apart at the seams.

I'd managed to take a few photos during the evening, and I used that as my excuse to sit down on the couch and show them to her, starting with the ones I took of Leah. My mom wouldn't be able to resist.

Devon had escorted Matilda home, and my dad stayed outside, clearing up the patio. It was just Mom and me, so now was the perfect time to ask a few questions.

"So, Mom, I'm curious. Is Devon an ex-con?" I reckoned I'd start high, aim low.

"Don't be ridiculous, Pip. Wherever did you get such an idea?"

"Well, you're asking me to keep all kinds of secrets from

him, so I figured it was, you know, to protect us." That should get me some answers.

"Oh, no, dear, it's to protect Devon." Well, that was unexpected.

"Protect him from what? Or who? Oh my god, is someone after Devon? Is someone blackmailing him too?"

"Of course not. My, you do have quite the imagination, don't you? You got that from me, you know." She chuckled, though nothing of this conversation was funny. "So. Pippa. Tell me. This thing with Devon. What's going on?"

"Thing?"

"Really, Pippa. Don't even try to deny it. I'm your mother."

I couldn't deny it, but that didn't mean I had any more idea than she did. "I don't have a clue, Mom. And before you say it, I'm not evading. I honestly don't know."

"Fair enough," she said softly. Then she smiled, that *mother-knows-everything* kind of smile. "Look, Pippa, I don't tell your father everything either. It's for his own good. Sometimes what he does know might hurt him. I can't allow that."

"Does Dad know about the money?"

"In a manner of speaking. He knows enough, just not all the gory details. And Pippa, one last thing. I know you're still sorting through this situation with Devon, just remember, nobody is perfect, but they might be perfect for you."

Who knew my mother had such words of wisdom to impart? Sure, they were pretty much a cliché, but she was right. I'd been waiting for some pie-in-the-sky fantasy guy. Time to change the subject back to my primary concern.

"So, this thing with Devon where I can't tell him anything. To protect him. You're going to have to clue me in. I'm not good at secrets, so I need to have a super good reason. Otherwise, all bets are off." There. Ultimatum time.

She gave me one of her studied looks—where she contemplated a whole host of issues in her head while looking at me through squinted eyes with her head tilted slightly upward. I stayed quiet as a church mouse, silently praying to the gods of mothers everywhere that she'd acquiesce. Thankfully, one of those gods answered my prayers. She glanced around. I assumed to make sure my dad was still outside.

"Pippa, we all agreed you shouldn't know this. It's for your own good. I'm sure you realize that."

"My having to keep secrets from Devon comes down to you having to keep secrets from me? The secrets *someone else* already knows? You really can't tell me?"

"I will, Pip, but not right now. It's for your own protection. It'll all be fine, I promise."

"If you want to wait to tell me, fine. But about Devon, out with it. He's not married, is he? No, that wouldn't prevent me from telling him. Honestly, Mom. Too many people are asking me not to tell their secrets, and I'm not sure I can keep doing that."

Mom must have seen my frustration because she sighed. "Okay, Pippa, I'll tell you why you must keep this from Devon because I see how you and he are together, but he mustn't know that you know."

"Know what? Out with it, Mom." Finally, I'd get some answers.

"Yes, Kate, know what?" My heart skipped a beat at Devon's deep voice behind me.

"Devon, hello! Back so soon?" Mom asked, quite cheerfully.

"Yes, Devon, back so soon? Wait, why are you back?" I was *so* close. His timing sucked. On the bright side, it would be totally his fault I couldn't tell him anything.

"I thought I'd follow you home. Just in case." He looked at me so sweetly, I about melted.

"Oh, yes, dear, I think that's a good idea. Devon, how

thoughtful of you!" My mother sure could lay it on thick. I glared at her, then looked back at him. He had that *who me?* look of total innocence. I silently vowed that when we got to my place, that boy would get an earful. I was sure he knew what my mom knew that I didn't—and it was driving me crazy.

However, considering I'd dressed to the nines and didn't want to waste any of it, I stood slowly and gracefully, then leaned over to give my mother a kiss on the cheek as I said good night ever so sweetly. I took a moment to grab my tripod and camera, then headed to my car while doing my best runway walk. Devon didn't say a word. He just got in his car, waited for me to back out, and followed me home. I figured he was going to come in. Truthfully, I was looking forward to it and dreading it all at once.

Assuming Devon would be right behind me, I parked my car in my driveway, then proceeded to the front door. I didn't look back until I'd let myself into my house—and was just in time to see him simply drive off.

Are you freaking kidding me?

I stood in my darkened front room and shook my head in disbelief. Had I totally misread all the signals? Impossible. Had I given off bad vibes? Again, impossible. Something was terribly awry. My whole approach that night screamed, "take me, I'm yours," yet he'd driven away. The Tarot cards were quite obviously wrong. Somehow deep down, I should have known.

I put my stuff down, and my phone buzzed.

Devon: Night, Red. Sweet Dreams.

I'd begun to think someone had plucked me out of my life and deposited me in one of those predictably sappy but addictive Hallmark movies—the ones I watched even though I knew I'd end up ugly crying on the couch with a glass of wine, a bag of popcorn, and a box of tissues.

Work the next day was a welcome reprieve. There was always something to do in an antique store, and it was a way to keep my mind focused on something other than Luckland's crime spree—and way, way off Devon. There were so many fabulous items to look at, research, and dust off. I kept busy most of the day. When I finally took a break to check my email and blog traffic, I found that traffic was up over a thousand percent, which was a surprise. I checked the analytics; Nature's Future had linked to my blog, which meant a ton more readers and hopefully more followers. I was over the moon. Having the environmental group's backing was the first big step in pitching an actual paid gig. Rumor had it they were looking to do an entire climate change series featuring the impact on Colorado's indigenous species—and it would require several feature photographers. My wildflower blooms had their attention. Now I just had to capitalize on it. It may not have been the Sierra Club, but I needed to start somewhere.

First, I tweeted out their article with my embedded link before sharing it on Instagram and Facebook. Then I ran up front to tell my dad. I knew he'd be excited for me, but he had a customer, so I headed to the back and looked for my mom, but there was no sign of her. I sighed. Nothing was more frustrating than bursting with good news and having nobody to share it with. I texted Dani, but she was probably somewhere on the floor of the Gulf of Mexico and wouldn't see my message for a while.

I hesitated a moment, then with my nerves strung a little tight, I texted Devon. Considering he'd ditched me the night before, I wasn't sure if he'd even respond, but I hoped he realized how important my news was to me.

He replied within seconds.

Devon: Congrats, Red! We'll celebrate. 7 p.m. Your place.

I hadn't expected that. Though exactly the response I wanted, I hadn't dared hope for it. I was now officially ecstatic and terrified all at once. I wasn't one for panic attacks, but if I were, I think I would have had one. I had a strange need for my mom again, which had become a habit, and thankfully, she arrived in the nick of time. She came in through the back, several shopping bags in hand, which was interesting. I couldn't see the name on the bags, but they certainly weren't groceries, and I wondered where she'd been.

"Mom. Advice. I need some." That would get her; it always did.

"But of course, Pippa. Come sit. Tell me." That was the mom I would do anything for. She wasn't always available, but when she was, I seized the moment.

I told her about my blog and how the environmental group had picked it up and that I'd shared on social media, which, of course, was way out of her league in terms of comprehension—but that was okay. She was happy for me because I was happy for me. Then I told her about Devon and his idea of celebrating. I also told her I was nervous, which was out of character. I hadn't been nervous since high school.

"Pippa, dear, you're nervous because you've finally let your guard down." Oh, that was good. She zeroed right in on the problem.

"Exactly. I can't afford to do that."

"You can't afford not to." She patted my knee before she took her things to the front. I was quite sure she cut the conversation off before I could ask about Devon again. Perceptive mother I had there, especially about my defensive attitude.

I decided to consult with Babs. Though talking to her about Devon was probably a bad idea, I also wanted to learn more about the Panello place and her new job, specifically if she'd been over there yet, and if she needed help. I could certainly do any photography she might need as I'd had plenty of experience shooting interior spaces for designers. I called her and held my breath until she answered.

"Babs, are you busy?"

"Of course I am, Pippa. Today is my first day of work. So naturally, I'm busy. But I will make time for you if it's important." She laid it on pretty thick, but whatever.

"I need advice."

"Well, why didn't you say so," she said, suddenly turning into the chipper good witch. "Come right over."

Clearly, my family was never more in their element than when giving advice or telling me what to do. I wasn't sure why. I was the normal one with common sense who was semi-independent, and career driven. Nevertheless, I headed over to my sister's *humble* home.

Being a few minutes outside of town, she and her husband had the luxury of acreage. Once upon a time, her house was a basic white colonial. Then, with a few renovations, including an entire third-floor addition, she had transformed it into a manor house—with a veranda, not a front porch, and a foyer, not just an entry. The upside of being on acreage meant it had a fabulous circular drive out front, so parking was easy. My place just had a little side gravel driveway that led directly to the ramshackle garage out back. Hers had a triple attached garage on the side with a separate driveway.

I used the brass knocker on the wooden double entry doors to announce my presence. All she needed was a butler, and the whole picture would be complete. Thankfully, Luckland didn't have butlers for hire, or she probably would have had one.

She ushered me into the gallery, which was what she called what used to be the living room. I glanced around, surprised.

She'd rearranged the entire room to have a sectioned-off area near the front with a desk and credenza. Almost like a home office.

"Like it, Pip? We had to set up a little office for me, and Tom thought this the perfect spot."

"I have to say, this is really charming. Well done. You've thought of everything, haven't you?"

"Well, I have to make this work. It's important."

"I know. And I'm here to support you. You know that."

I headed over to the couch, where I reminded myself *not* to get too comfortable. As in "putting my feet on the coffee table" comfortable. That was simply not allowed at Babs's house. She didn't even have a recliner, just those tufted high-back chairs that looked as if they were meant for high tea.

"Okay, Pip, what can I help you with? This is about Devon, I suppose." I swear that must be Luckland's only bit of gossip.

"Yes and no. Yes, it's about Devon but not totally the way you think. Why do you think we aren't allowed to tell him how Mom and the others found that money? If we can know because we're Mom's daughters, then as Tillie's son, why shouldn't he know?"

"I don't know. I asked Tom the same thing."

"You told Tom?" Actually, I wasn't surprised. I told Dani.

"Of course. He doesn't understand it either. I asked Mother, but she wouldn't say anything more. I do wonder if there isn't something else to the story than they're telling us."

"Well, considering the blackmail threats, clearly there is. Maybe I can somehow ask Devon tonight without getting specific—see if there's a reason the ladies would keep secrets from him?"

"Tonight! Oh, do tell, Pip!" Babs was now all ears.

"Okay, well, Nature's Future picked up my blog. I was so excited, but nobody was around, so I texted Devon. He texted back." I showed her the message thread on the phone, but I needed to make sure of one thing. "Nothing has happened between Devon and me. Not. A. Thing." That *had* to be clearly established.

"But you want something to happen, right? He's clearly a catch, hot as blazes, and he's obviously smitten. Always has been. He gave you a cat. Who wouldn't fall for that?"

Smitten? Hot as blazes? Only Babs could talk like that. *Wait, what?*

"What do you mean he's always been smitten?"

"Oh, please. How could you be so blind?"

I didn't think I was blind, but that didn't make Babs all seeing either. "He lives in Virginia."

"But you want to see him again." Between Babs and my mom, they seemed to have had me pegged.

"So, what do I do?" I asked point-blank. My gut reaction was to flee and head for the hills—literally.

"I think you know the answer, Pippa. It's time you took the plunge. You're the fearless one, remember?"

I wasn't so sure about that. Right about then, I wasn't sure about anything.

CHAPTER EIGHTEEN

Since I'd already worn the little black dress, I spent a great deal of time looking for the next best thing. Given that there *was* no next best thing, I settled for a low-cut V-neck sweater and leggings. Simple and sexy. At least, that was what I was going for.

Seven o'clock couldn't come fast enough. I was ready at six. I fiddled with my laptop, then fluffed the pillows on the couch. After that, I tidied up the kitchen then sat and stared at the recliner. When I checked the time, it was only a quarter past six. It was absurd. I was not sixteen waiting for a date to the prom.

The doorbell rang at precisely seven—as if Devon had stood out there waiting for exactly the right time. I wouldn't have put it past him. I peeked out the window, then opened the door.

He stood on the porch, looking almost as nervous as I felt— and bearing gifts. He carried a bottle of wine, a basket, and a large bunch of flowers. Not roses, tulips, or daffodils though. He'd brought wildflowers from the meadow. I was sure there wasn't a woman alive that could resist Devon right then. I certainly couldn't.

Grinning like an idiot, I took the flowers, then led him into the kitchen. From the aromas, the basket held something delicious. "What's for dinner?"

Devon smiled. "I've no idea. Hope and Marcy packed this for us."

The divas' involvement might have dampened the mood, but Devon's enthusiasm curtailed my annoyance.

"Go ahead, Pip, you sit. I've got this." He pulled out the chair for me and winked.

I sat and took deep breaths, trying to settle my racing pulse. I watched as he carefully began unpacking the basket, which definitely held some of the Blue Sky Café's finest creations, and I couldn't help but smile when I noticed my favorite cheesecake.

Once he had everything laid out, he opened the wine and poured us each a glass, then sat across from me. He really did look a lot like Jon Bon Jovi. The variances were Devon's height, chiseled features, and neatly trimmed hair that differed from the infamous long-haired eighties locks. I wondered how I'd never noticed the resemblance. I'd listened to a lot of Bon Jovi as a tween, especially with Matilda's penchant for singing their songs every karaoke night.

"Maybe we should eat?" Devon smiled, and I was sure my heart skipped a beat.

I nodded but somehow couldn't look away. The air around us practically sizzled, so did my blood. I needed to put some brakes on. "So, Dev. If you could pick one place to go where you'd never been, where would it be?"

Devon's eyes lit up. "Easy. Athens. Remember our tenth-grade social studies project?"

"You built the Parthenon and came to class in a toga. Mr. Jensen laughed so hard he spat out his coffee. Who could forget?" I smiled at the memory.

Devon chuckled, then began putting food on his plate. "What about you?"

"Ireland. Most definitely."

"Ireland would suit you."

"Why?" I wondered if he was back to the old Devon—ready with a quip.

"I heard it's a photographer's dream."

I blinked because I really hadn't expected his response. "It is." I watched him for a moment, then smiled. "Are you going to eat the rest of those sesame noodles?" I noticed he was heaping them on his plate.

"Sorry, did you want some?"

I laughed. "You know I do. Pass them over. The only thing I like better than Hope and Marcy's sesame noodles and cheesecake is their chocolate soufflé."

"I'll remember that for next time."

So, this wouldn't be a once-only deal. A flush heated my cheeks, but I held Devon's gaze. "Okay. Next time we'll get pizza. You'll have to up your toppings game though."

"We'll go half and half. I'll try yours, and you try mine. Now, tell me about the project. The blog. What happened?"

For a second, my thoughts had gone to trying out Devon, but then I mentally shook my head. "Well, Nature's Future reviewed my post and featured a link to it. Traffic went up a zillion, and now I have a thousand new followers. Also, the environmental group offered me a slot on their upcoming major climate change project."

He raised his glass and pierced me with a look I couldn't really pinpoint—it was as if he were saying far more than words would convey.

"Well, cheers to you, Pippa. You, of all people, deserve this."

"I do?"

"It makes you happy, yeah?"

I nodded.

"Then yeah, you do."

"Thanks. That means a lot to me."

We clinked glasses, and I took a long sip of wine before I dove into our sumptuous meal. We ate in silence while I sneaked glances at him when I could. Occasionally, our glances would meet, and we'd lock gazes for a moment.

"Can I ask you something, Devon?"

"Anything."

"Do you think you'll try to track down your father? You have his name, right?"

"I do. Trey Marks. Matilda didn't use a fake name on the certificate. I assumed she expected or hoped I'd find out someday."

"So, will you look for him?"

"I think I might, yes. I'm sure Mom wants me to."

I smiled and lifted my glass. "Here's to a successful search."

"Speaking of, Red, how about you give me the glasses you swiped last night. I've got a buddy who can dust them for prints. See what the IAFIS can pull up."

"The whatzit?"

"Sorry, the Integrated Automated Fingerprint Identification System."

"Fancy acronym you have there. Is that something available to private investigators?" I really wanted a definitive answer on that because I simply wanted answers on Devon. I held my breath as he paused.

"It's available to my buddy," he replied.

I inwardly sighed. I should have known he'd be evasive. I retrieved the glasses, then gave them to him. He placed them in the basket, then carefully began clearing off the table. When he had everything put away, and there was nothing left to do, he shoved his hands in his pant pockets.

"I guess you'll be off then?" I asked. I wanted to ask whether he wanted to stay, but I couldn't bring myself to take that step. Looking at the furrow between his eyes, I didn't think he could either, though I was almost sure he would have stayed if I'd asked.

"I have an early start tomorrow," he said, his voice huskier than usual.

His answer didn't mean he was going to leave, but it also didn't mean he was going to stay. I held his gaze, willing him to make a move.

He picked up the basket.

Crushing disappointment sat like a heavy stone on my chest, but unwilling to let him know how I felt, I headed to the front door, vaguely aware that he followed me.

"Pippa…"

I turned and caught his expression, which seemed to convey the same regret as the one filling my heart.

"I really have to leave early tomorrow. Any other time…"

I nodded, not sure I believed him, but then he dropped the basket, and with a deep groan, he placed his palms on my cheeks and pressed his lips to mine with a fierceness I didn't expect. I gasped, and he instantly slid his tongue against mine. God, he smelled so good, and he tasted divine, and when I pressed my hands against his chest, I couldn't help but notice how solid he was. He wrapped his arms around me, and I found out how solid he was in other areas too…

A million thoughts flashed through my mind; the most dominant was for him not to stop. Not ever.

Slowly, he pulled back, leaving a tiny kiss on the edge of my mouth. I shivered and almost clutched at his arms, wanting them back around me, but he put some distance between us for both our sakes. Tonight wasn't going to be the night he stayed over. His eyes glittered in the porch light as he tilted his lips into a smile. "Night, Red." He picked up the basket, then left.

I watched him go, then went back inside. Almost on automatic, I locked the door and set the alarm. It wasn't until I'd sat on my recliner with 99 in my lap that I grinned.

I'd always believed kissing to be an intimate act, and as first kisses went, it was pretty spectacular. It also erased any doubt that Devon and I were destined to be together. Maybe the Tarot cards weren't so wrong after all.

The following morning, I woke up to a text.

Devon: See you soon. Stay safe.

Stay safe? With the super-sized deluxe alarm in my house, I felt incredibly safe—unless Devon wasn't telling me something. Maybe his reasons for leaving were to do with the boxes and the Panellos. Hopefully, he could sort it all out soon. In the meantime, I had a pitch to work on and a career to further.

I was about to grab breakfast, but my phone buzzed.

Babs: Pip! Hurry. Mother's house. Now.

My sister's emergency texts were getting ridiculous, but like a dutiful daughter and sister, I went.

When I got there, voices lured me to the patio, where I found the posse plus Babs immersed in an animated discussion or verbal warfare. Everyone was talking at once in increasingly louder voices. They needed a time-out, so I stuck two fingers in my mouth and whistled.

Silence ensued—along with a few glares.

"Okay, one of you and only one of you, please explain." I almost sounded like Devon just then.

"The lasagna recipe. It's gone viral," said Hope with a dramatic sigh.

"Which is why we've been slammed all week with lasagna diners," Marcy said, adding her own dramatic flair.

"What do you mean, viral? You posted your recipe online?" That clearly was a bad idea.

"Of course they didn't, but someone did," my mother said. "And it's a disaster!"

"But who and why? Who has the recipe besides you two?" I asked Hope and Marcy.

Marcy glanced at Hope. "No one, other than my aunt Hilda, and she definitely wouldn't leak the lasagna recipe, or any recipe for that matter."

"So, you think someone stole it? It's good, yes, bordering on insanely delicious, but good enough to *steal?*"

"Pippa, that lasagna would melt the tongue off any critic in the country, and you know it," said Matilda.

Just to verify they weren't all destined for the loony bin, I pulled my phone from my pocket and googled lasagna.

Just outside Denver, best lasagna ever found.

The secret to perfect lasagna, unveiled in the Rockies.

Want to serve perfect lasagna? Try this secret recipe from the Blue Sky Café!

The ladies weren't kidding, and they weren't crazy. Someone had clearly revealed their recipe online, and it had become newsworthy. Damn. While the publicity was good for business, they'd lost control over their super-secret recipe.

"We need to get that taken down," said my mom. "Right away."

"Sorry, Mom, no can do. The internet doesn't work that way. Once it's there, it's there. All we can hope is that more people will come to try the original than bake it themselves— and that no other restaurant begins putting it on their menu."

All the women reacted as I thought they would, with lots of hand fluttering, muttering, and general disappointment.

"We need to be proactive, ladies." I definitely sounded like Devon, but without him around, I needed to step up. "It's time the Blue Sky Café became social. We need an Instagram account and a few posts. We also need to make sure if things go viral. it's because you want them to."

Everyone nodded in agreement, then looked at me expectantly. I sighed. "Yes, I'll take care of it. I'll set it up and get you started, but then you have to manage it yourselves, deal?"

With their crisis temporarily averted, there were smiles all around as the ladies stood and began their goodbyes. Then Hope and Marcy's phones went off. By their expressions as they looked at their screens, it was not good news.

"There's been an explosion at the café," Hope whispered, her voice quaking.

"We have to go," said Marcy.

Things were turning scary as hell, and I immediately, instinctively, texted Devon.

Me: Get to the café, quick!

I only hoped he wasn't too far away.

CHAPTER NINETEEN

WE RACED INTO THE CAFÉ, ONLY TO FIND DEVON AND RANDY, THE sous chef, lounging by the counter and laughing.

"What's happened? Randy, you said there was an explosion?" Marcy looked baffled as if she didn't understand what could be funny. I glared at Devon, wondering how he could have gotten there before us.

"Sorry, ladies," Randy replied, his soft tone belying his large frame. "Seems one of your vintage bubblies was a bit too bubbly and popped its cork."

Devon shook his head and chuckled, then gave me a light nod before he slipped out the back door. I would have been quite happy going after him because his being here meant he'd never left town. When he told me he was leaving and had an early start, I assumed he was off somewhere, so what was he up to? Once again, Devon Marks was acting cagey.

Before I could really get a good mad on, Babs came over.

"Why don't we head to my new job site?"

"Job site?"

"Yes. Panello Palace."

I'd forgotten I promised to help by going to the Panello house with her. "What did you call it?"

"Panello Palace. You know, on HGTV, they always name the houses they renovate. Even the tiny ones. Last night they had the Little Lamb Cottage episode. Looked more like a trailer, but I'm not the expert."

The obviousness of that statement had me shaking my head. The old Tindle house was one of a kind. No one had lived in it for years. The last owner passed over to the great beyond, leaving it to his son, who nobody had ever met. Most people around town never met old man Tindle either. In a town our size, that was virtually impossible. *Someone* had to have run into him at least once or twice. Hence the stories that surrounded the estate.

"I'll drive us," Babs said as we headed onto the sidewalk.

I noticed my mom following close behind with Matilda, Prudence, and Hope. "Are they coming too?"

"Of course. The more help, the better."

I wondered how the Panello boys would react to this invasion. "Are the brothers going to be there?" I hoped they weren't. They really creeped me out, and I vacillated between thinking they were stalkers and circus refugees.

"Oh, my no, Pippa, they most certainly aren't in residence at the moment. Not with all the work I need to do. They've secured rooms at the Inn for a few days."

I wondered if that meant rooms had opened up at the Inn or if the Panellos were stuck with the one Devon and I had the misfortune of sharing. It wouldn't have surprised me if Freddie and Frankie felt at home there, and I thought about telling Babs about the red satin sheets, the lace doilies, and a fake bear rug, but she was simply too serious about this job, so I kept it to myself. When I next saw Devon, however, I knew he'd see the same hilarity I did. Or was I getting too ahead of myself? The kiss last night was amazing, but the fact he hadn't left town, as he'd said, left me feeling a little unsure of where I stood with him.

We drew up to the house, and once we'd all gathered at the entrance, Babs smiled. "I'm going to give you a tour so you can see the challenges ahead of us."

Us? She was the one getting paid for this job—*we* were not. I wasn't sure she quite understood the concept of employment yet.

My phone buzzed, and I grabbed it to distract myself.

Devon: Look for the boxes while you're in there.

That was kind of spooky. How did he know *exactly* where I was? He'd definitely installed a tracking device on my phone, or he followed me, or had someone else follow me. The question was why? Did he not trust me, or did he think the Panellos were into something more sinister than the stolen Vegas money? A very odd vibe surrounded Devon sometimes, and I wondered if it had anything to do with his job as a PI or whether he simply liked acting secretive. He often behaved as if he had something to hide, like someone with secrets. Unfortunately, I had no time to consider what was going on with him because I had a tour to take.

The women were about as excited as they could be, especially Prudence. I was beginning to think she had a thing for those two buffoons; I just wasn't sure which one, as neither was very appealing.

The house itself was unusual, an old stone manor, rather gothic, which I found really intriguing and very cool—exactly the one I would buy given a chance. The two-bedroom crafts-man-style cottage I rented was cute but didn't compare to the drama of a gothic manor. Truth was, I was curious to hear my sister's plans for the place and hoped she could see the char-acter in it and not want to change the home's integrity. When I walked in, I marveled at the massively wide mahogany stairs with the worn, totally authentic red carpet. To the right, French doors led to the dining room, and to the left, another set of French doors opened to the sitting room. In some respects, it reminded me of a house in which a Jane Austen heroine would have lived. In other ways, Count Dracula. I eagerly listened as Babs explained what she wanted to do, and I nodded my approval about a third of the way into her spiel. She wasn't going to change a thing. She would just bring out the character and add a bit of modern flair. Precisely what I would do—if it were mine.

As we got to the main bedroom, I heard my phone buzz once more. Several texts arrived one after the other.

Devon: Check the closets.

Devon: Don't forget the basement.

Devon: Look in the pantry and the mud room.

No way could he know if there was a mud room or a pantry unless he'd somehow unearthed blueprints. Regardless, my problem was trying to snoop without making it appear as if I was snooping. If the ladies found out what I was doing, they'd go ballistic. They obviously had no clue the Panellos may not be legit.

I made a few gallant attempts to check all the nooks and crannies upstairs while waxing lyrical about the period fixtures. Babs smiled at my enthusiasm, which wasn't all baloney, but as we headed back down the stairs without me spotting a thing, the aforementioned buffoons arrived.

"Well, hello, ladies! How are we today?" Freddie, the tall one, asked. His strange falsetto echoed in the cavernous foyer.

"Oh, we're splendid," Prudence said. She smiled coyly. "Aren't we, girls?" She looked at each of us, daring us not to agree.

Then the short one, Frankie, cleared his throat. "Why don't we have tea in the parlor? If you'll follow me?"

Though it would be rude to say no, I thought his request quite odd. They acted as if we had come to see them rather than returning home to find us there. Still, we piled into the parlor, where all the chairs sat in one corner. I assumed Babs had put them that way because she would be working there. I started to pull a chair away from the wall when Freddie became surly.

"No, no, just sit. Why don't you all sit?" He didn't make it a question though. He made it a command.

I immediately knew something wasn't right, but before I could react, Frankie locked the French doors while Freddie pulled out a gun. He waved it toward the chairs.

"Sit."

Hope didn't move—she seemed to be stuck to the floor. My mother began fluttering her hands like a baby bird trying to take flight, Matilda stomped her foot like a child close to a tantrum, and Prudence pulled a flask out of her blazer pocket and took some long swigs.

Babs looked at me in the way twins did. There was a whole lot in that look. We could defend ourselves, but not when there were four other women to protect. Still, I read her loud and clear. She stepped forward and faced the two men, hands on her hips, and started blathering on. I had no clue what she said, and I was sure they didn't either, but while she distracted them, I slowly headed toward the chairs while I searched in my sweatshirt pocket for my phone. Using the finger sensor on the back, I silently prayed the phone would unlock. The buzz confirmed it did. Then I tried my damnedest to picture the screen with the icon for Devon. Bottom right. I tapped around on the bottom right until the phone vibrated. I had no idea if I'd got the right app, but I could only hope since I had a hunch there wouldn't be another chance.

Freddie began waving his damn gun around again. I sat and yanked my mom down next to me on one side and Matilda on the other. Prudence, Hope, and Babs quickly followed.

"Now then," he said. "Where is it?"

If anyone had dropped a pin, I would have heard it. I had a good idea what he was talking about, but the ladies, including Babs, had no clue that Devon and I had earmarked the Panellos as less than honorable men who possibly had something to do with the Vegas heist. Seemed we were right.

"Don't ignore me. Where is it?" Freddie asked in that horrible high-pitched voice.

"Where is what?" I needed to know for sure what he wanted. I also needed to give Devon time to get here.

"Don't play dumb," he said. "Where's the money?"

The ladies on either side of me stopped breathing.

"I've no idea what money you're talking about. If you believe you've been overcharged for the items you bought at the store, perhaps you should speak to my father, but this is certainly no way—"

A low growl ripped from Freddie's throat. "I'm talking about the money they took from us." He nodded at the four older ladies. "They know. Ask them. They know."

Well, okey dokey, then. I sighed dramatically as if fed up with the accusations. "Ladies, do you know where Mr. Panello's money is?"

My mother spoke first. "I'm sure we do not know what on earth this man is talking about." The way she said it, she sounded bored.

Frankie glanced at his brother, then seemed to decide it was his turn to push for answers. "Look, ladies, we know you have it. We saw you take it. It's time to return what's ours."

"Why on earth do you think we have any money of yours?" Hope asked, her tone as mild as my mother's. God, these ladies were good.

"Because." Freddie sneered. "We saw you. That night. Vegas? 1989? Ringing any bells, girls?"

At that point, I didn't even think *I* was breathing. So, the brothers were in Vegas at the time of the robbery and wanted the money they believed the ladies had. As far as I was concerned, the Panellos had just admitted they robbed the casino. Now all I had to do was get them to confess.

"Eighty-nine? Oh, that was a fine trip, wasn't it, girls?" Matilda's smile was whimsical. "That was truly a fine, fine trip."

I doubted she'd recalled the money, the dark alley, or their race back to the hotel. She'd probably thought of Devon's dad— or she was a far better actress than I ever gave her credit for.

"You stole our money, and now it's time to give it back." Frankie puffed up like a blowfish and began pacing.

"Yours? Yours? You robbed a casino. So technically, it's not yours at all," Prudence declared.

The rest of the ladies gave a collective groan. So far, the brothers hadn't said a word about the casino, but Prudence being Prudence, let it all fly. I had an inkling her flask was empty.

"How do you know we stole anything? You know nothing!" Freddie practically spat out the words. If he weren't waving a gun around, the situation would have been quite funny—in a dark sort of way.

I told myself not to panic—the situation was too surreal for that. Besides, too many people knew where we were. The Panellos must not have realized how idiotic holding us hostage was, and what were they going to do if we didn't talk? Shoot us?

Uncomfortable with where my thoughts had taken me, I glanced at the ladies, who didn't seem all that nervous. Quite the opposite, they seemed overly calm as if this were just any old day in Luckland.

That was when I stared at Babs, willing her to look at me. When she did, she smiled. There were times being a twin had benefits, and that was one of them. I nodded to tell her I had this. Though, to be truthful, I had no idea if I did. I was certainly going to give it a go, however.

CHAPTER TWENTY

As I tried to figure out what I could do, my phone rang with quite possibly the most obnoxious, loudest ringtone ever—the theme from the Lone Ranger. Everybody stared at me. I figured answering would be out of the question, so I ignored it. However, I knew who was calling. Devon. I cracked a smile because only he would have chosen a ringtone like that for himself. His call also meant he'd gotten my signal, and the cavalry was on its way. So, all I had to do was keep the crazy man with the gun from firing it.

Frankie curled his lip. "Something funny, Miss Pippi?"

"That's Pippa to you, Frankie Furter." I gritted my teeth, trying to restrain my temper. Though unwise to provoke him, I couldn't control my irritation at his snide tone.

My mom clucked her tongue. "Pippa, mind your manners, please."

A guy had a gun pointed at us, and Mom thought to correct *my* manners? Granted, I understood her concerns.

"Sorry," I said. "You know how I get when I'm hungry." I wasn't hungry, but it seemed an excellent way to change the course of our conversation and waste time. "I don't suppose there's food around?"

"Yes, Frankie, you did promise us tea," Prudence said, her tone edged with artful seduction. I wasn't sure if she was playing with him or genuinely still thought she was in with a chance. Either way, whatever happened next ought to be good.

I looked at Frankie to gauge his reaction. He seemed to consider her request, and though I thought it implausible, people were odd creatures.

"Ms. Prudence, my apologies." He glanced at his brother, who glared.

"Shut up, Frankie," Freddie said. "She can eat when we get our money."

Seemed we were at a stalemate. The ladies weren't giving anything away, and the brothers didn't seem to know how to get them to talk. We all stared at one another. Freddie's arm had to be getting tired, and I wondered how long he could keep it up.

My phone rang again. I didn't know what kind of app that man installed on my phone, but Melissa Etheridge sang about a window. Devon didn't have to hit me over the head with a sledgehammer; I got it. I just had to figure out how to accomplish what he wanted.

"It's getting a bit toasty in here. Perhaps you could open a window? You don't want anyone fainting, do you?"

Babs glanced at me, and I gave her a short nod to let her know I had a plan.

"Frankie, go open that window, but not more than a few inches. You hear me?"

"Loud and clear," he muttered. He definitely showed some resentment as he came over and reached behind me to unlock the window a bare minimum, then he returned to stand next to his lanky brother. They made a ridiculous pair.

"Now, ladies, let's try this again." Freddie sounded less nasty, but that high-pitched twangy voice reminded me of nails on a chalkboard.

"Where is the money?" He spoke as if we were disobedient children. I thought about sending them off on a wild goose chase, but I had a hunch they'd end up taking us with them. Even though they appeared dumb as lampposts, I didn't want to take that chance.

"Excuse me, please explain why you think these sweet old ladies have your money?" I played the ignorant card, hoping it would work. I also wanted to know how the Panellos thought the ladies could access funds while we were all sitting here. Even if the ladies caved and agreed to give the Panellos some money, which I couldn't see happening, there was no way to get cash of any value. The ladies had told me they'd invested their ill-gotten gains, and it would be almost impossible to transfer any stocks, or whatever they had, without lots of paperwork. The Panellos obviously hadn't seen their idea through. Imbeciles. Could it be they thought the money still sat in bags in the ladies' houses? Under their beds or somewhere?

"Did we not just explain that? We saw them!" replied Frankie.

"Just who are you calling old, Pip," said Prudence. "We most certainly are not old."

I glared at Pru. The woman genuinely didn't get the severity of the situation.

"I honestly don't understand why you think you saw these women thirty years ago," I said. "They clearly don't look a bit like their young selves." I risked exile for that last remark, but I'd take that risk if it got us out of there.

Freddie snorted. "Of course they don't, but we've been looking for them for years."

Frankie nodded. "That's right, and if we hadn't run into that professor, we'd still be looking."

Prudence gasped, and my mother sucked in a sharp breath. Freddie glared at Frankie, and Matilda and Hope looked stunned. Their reactions at the mention of a professor sure made him important. I was quietly figuring out how to ask who he was when a faint whisper behind me caught my ear.

"Hey, Red."

I had never, ever in my entire life, been so glad to hear those words. I held my breath, hoping for more.

"Distract them," Devon whispered.

Easier said than done, but I was nothing if not inventive. I did the first thing any woman in my shoes would do. "Excuse me, Freddie. I'm gonna need to pee." At least it worked in third grade.

The two misfits looked at each other in horror while I, with a most innocent expression, waited with legs crossed. For good measure, I did a few bounces—the "I gotta go" dance.

My mother nodded approvingly, Matilda cracked a smile, and Hope glanced at me while Prudence took another swig from her flask. Seemed it wasn't empty after all. Babs tilted her chin in a way I knew all too well.

"Me too," she said.

"Okay," Frankie said after a confirming nod from Freddie. "Come with me. No funny stuff. You try anything, and Freddie will put a hole right between those pretty eyes."

I almost laughed at him—Frankie Panello, aka Scarface.

Babs and I stood with a slight nod of acknowledgment. Her thoughts were definitely alongside mine, though I wasn't sure our idea would actually work. What we planned, we'd only tried twice in our lives, neither time too successfully—once when Billy Jasper teased Lena Harper in the playground, and the second time when Devon pulled the head off one of my Ken dolls. I quickly wondered if he remembered the doll incident. I bet he did. Anyway, third time's the charm, and I guessed we were about to find out.

As we followed Frankie into the entryway and around the corner by the stairs, Babs and I looked at each other. She went right, I went left, and we each grabbed one of Frankie's elbows while we kicked out his legs. Frankie landed flat on his back. A perfect slam dunk. Babs quickly put her hand over his mouth while I had the privilege of sitting on him. Truthfully, it worked a lot easier when we were kids, but we succeeded in our goal. Freddie must have heard the loud thud, but if he investigated, there'd be no one to hold a gun on the ladies. Divide and conquer—which, when someone had a gun, only worked if the cavalry arrived.

The front door burst open, and the sheriff, a few deputies, Devon, and several guys I'd never seen before whose jackets said FBI, flooded in. The cavalry. Everything happened so fast I barely registered it. They all seemed to scatter about, every so often yelling, "Clear!" I hadn't moved. Neither had Babs. Frankie, however, squirmed and squealed like a pig. The sheriff and a few others came over, guns drawn, and told us we could get up.

Babs and I reluctantly obeyed, then went to see how our mom and the other ladies were doing. They were all talking over one another like in a scene from a made-for-TV movie. Realizing I wasn't going to get a word in edgewise, I looked for Devon and spotted him wearing one of those FBI jackets. From how it fit, I was pretty confident he hadn't borrowed it, and the way he spoke to the other agents, all authoritative and confident, told me Devon Marks had kept one hell of a secret from me.

His previous actions now kind of made sense, but I wasn't sure how to process. I suddenly felt like I had after someone had broken into my house—after the adrenaline rush had ebbed and awareness had set in.

I needed to get out of there, but the deputies had started taking statements. Frustrated, I waited my turn, a little mollified when my dad showed up with Tom. I figured Babs must have called them.

During the next few hours, none of us mentioned Vegas. Not a chance. In a tacit agreement, we all stated we had no idea why Frankie and Freddie had held us at gunpoint. I think the ladies assumed the Panellos wouldn't mention the Vegas heist or demanding money because that would mean incriminating themselves, but the brothers wouldn't get away with holding us hostage.

One more thing I realized during those hours was none of the divas raised as much as an eyebrow at the revelation that Devon was an FBI agent. Obviously, they already knew, and probably why I wasn't supposed to tell him about the money. Over the last few days, I'd become a sort of patsy in a bigger game they'd all played. An overwhelming sense of betrayal blurred my vision when I looked up and caught Devon staring at me. He hadn't interviewed anyone, probably because of his association with us. Didn't matter. I didn't want to talk to him anyway.

Finally allowed to leave, and needing a quiet place to think, I headed home. However, before I even had a chance to sit and relax, the doorbell rang. I knew who it was without even looking, though I hadn't thought he'd be so brazen as to come and see me so soon.

I opened the door, and Devon walked in. He put down a large bag and shut the door behind him. For long seconds he stared at me. I supposed he tried to judge my anger level, but before I could show him, he yanked me into his arms and kissed me.

I should have kicked him in the nether regions. Instead, I melted against his chest like Bridget Jones when she finally locked lips with Mark Darcy.

Slowly, Devon pulled back. "Are you okay?" he asked, his voice low and soothing, which did amazing things to help reduce my simmering resentment.

"No, I'm not okay. You could have let me know you were part of the FBI or something. Keeping me in the dark like that is pretty mean."

"I couldn't tell you, Pip. There was too much at stake, and before you say anything, it wasn't because I didn't trust you."

I sighed then turned and headed into the kitchen. I needed coffee. Devon followed with the bag, which he put on the counter. When he opened it and showed me its contents, my hostility evaporated a little more.

I made coffee for both of us, then sat at the counter. Devon sat opposite me, and I munched on one of Devon's chocolate chunk macadamia cookies while I contemplated how to bring up the fact he was FBI. In the end, a direct approach seemed the most appropriate. "So, why couldn't you tell me you were an agent before I had a gun waved in my face? I mean, everyone else knew."

"No one else was supposed to know. Yes, I told Tillie when I joined the FBI years ago, but I told her not to tell anyone. Seems she can't help telling her friends everything. I'm sorry, Red. I wanted to tell you, but I was undercover. I just couldn't risk it, and we had no idea the Panellos would do anything remotely like that. You know I'd never let anything happen to you."

"You knew who they were all along, then? That they stole the money from the casino?"

"We suspected, but we don't have any proof. We've been keeping an eye on them for a while but couldn't pin anything on them. Then they suddenly turned up in Luckland—"

"Looking for the money the ladies found."

"Yes, seems so. However, we didn't know the brothers had *lost* half the money, so we had no idea why they were here."

"But you figured it out when you saw the newspaper clipping and the picture of Hope and Prudence with the carpetbag full of money."

Devon grimaced. "Yes, which was a bit of a shock."

"That's an understatement." I took a sip of my coffee and eyed Devon. He played with a few crumbs on the counter. I could sense those cogs working in his brain again, and I imagined he was trying to put together a way of prosecuting the Panellos for their involvement in the Vegas heist. I didn't want to disturb him, but something was bothering me.

"When you searched the Panellos' house, did you find the boxes they bought?"

"No, which worries me, but we'll get a chance to ask about them tomorrow."

I absorbed that bit of information for a minute. "I've just thought of something. We are assuming the Panellos were the ones who threatened the ladies with their secrets, but the Panellos asked for the money as if they thought the ladies had bundles of cash hidden somewhere. However, if the brothers had opened the boxes, they would have known from the paperwork the money was invested and not easily accessible. So, I don't think they opened the boxes, and if they didn't, they couldn't have been the person who issued those threats because whoever threatened the ladies knows more than one secret hidden in those boxes. Remember, the blackmailer said, 'I know your secrets.' Plural. Therefore, I think the Panellos must have dumped the boxes without ever opening them, and now, someone else has them." Quite proud of my reasoning, though not of my conclusion, I watched Devon's reaction. He gave me a slight smile.

"I always knew you were smart. Yes, I think you're right. It's a logical explanation."

"So, what's next? There are still shoeboxes to find, and there is still someone out there who is threatening to reveal the ladies' secrets."

Devon frowned. "The person only said they knew the ladies' secrets, not that they would reveal them. As far as you and I know, they haven't asked for money or anything else to keep the secrets, which is certainly odd."

I would have agreed with him, but everything to do with the ladies seemed to be odd recently.

"I'd like to convene a meeting of the divas. Just for my own sake," he said.

I bit back a smile at his use of the word convene. "Agreed, but not tonight."

"No, not tonight." He stood and pulled me up with him. "Movie?"

"My choice." No way would I settle for Marvel comic heroes.

"But of course." The light in Devon's eyes came back before he dragged me over to the couch where he wrapped an arm around me. He even handed me the remote.

I scrolled through the romcoms and chick flicks, skipped right past the scary stuff, thought about comedy, nixed the steamy ones, and finally settled on a cooking show.

"Dev?"

"Yeah?" he whispered as he slid his fingers up and down my arm.

"How do you always know where I am? You're either very intuitive or have some inside info." I looked up at him and smiled. "You're tracking me, aren't you? One of those fancy apps on my phone, perhaps?"

"Just looking out for you, Pip. I take care of my own." He

kissed the top of my head. "Now pay attention, this guy makes magic with mushrooms."

I smiled and shook my head. The only magic I was concerned with was the kind Devon and I could make. However, it would have to wait.

I wasn't sure when I fell asleep, but when I awoke, my head lay on his chest. His heartbeat resounded in my ears, and I listened to its steady rhythm for a while before I realized he was absently combing his fingers through my hair. I held my breath, uncertain if I should move, but Devon must have sensed I was awake, and he shifted slightly.

"Morning, Red."

His nickname for me was not the best way to start my day, but it was growing on me.

"Morning, 007."

"Best you could do, huh?"

"Working on it." With that, I extricated myself from what was such a comfortable place, I wished I could have stayed there all day, but there were things to do.

CHAPTER TWENTY-ONE

After enjoying another delightful breakfast cooked by Devon, I let him do the honors of reaching out to the posse. I gave him a quick kiss then handed him his cell phone.

"Better gather the troops," I said.

He dialed Matilda first. I leaned forward expectantly. Would he greet her as Aunt Tillie? Matilda? Mom? She answered after two rings.

"Hello?"

"Good morning." Devon looked at me and grinned.

I leaned back and sighed. He did that on purpose.

"Devon, dear, good morning. How is Pippa today?"

I glanced at him. I couldn't tell if he wanted Matilda to know he'd stayed over. Not that we did anything last night that anyone could misconstrue, but the fact it was kind of early in the morning would be enough to have tongues wagging. Devon raised an eyebrow to show he'd give me the option of revealing my presence.

"I'm fine, Tillie. How are you doing this morning?"

"Just fine, luvvie. It's a beautiful morning, don't you think?"

Considering what we'd been through yesterday, she sounded awfully cheerful.

"I'm going to dial everyone in," Devon said. "We need to arrange a little chat." He pushed a few buttons and set the phone on the counter. The ladies seemed to answer all at once as if expecting the call.

"Hello?" My mom sounded a bit out of it, which Tillie was quick to pick up on.

"Kate, is that you? Goodness, you sound a bit off. Did you have your coffee yet?"

"Kate, try that new Peruvian blend I dropped off," Pru said.

"I did, Pru, but I think it's decaf."

"It's worse than decaf, Kate. Pru's joined one of those multi-level grifting coffee clubs again." Hope joined the conversation at that point. No greeting necessary. My head spun.

"Good morning, Hope, and I'm afraid you're right," my mom said. "Is Marcy there as well?"

"I'm here," she answered.

"Ladies, if I may?" Devon shook his head and smiled at me. "I've got you all on the line as we need to arrange to meet before you all chat with the sheriff this morning. I assume he's notified you all?"

"Affirmative," they said in unison. I wondered, not for the first time, if they could read one another's minds, and if they often used that skill to make things difficult for everyone around them. Arranging a simple meet-up should have been an easy task, but these women made turning a doorknob into a project.

"My house at eleven is just fine," said Matilda.

"Oh, dear, it'll have to be ten-thirty. I have a salon visit at eleven," said Prudence.

"Don't be silly, we'll meet at ten at my house," said my mom.

"I'm afraid Marcy and I have plans today, so it'll have to be nine," said Hope.

"Well, why don't we go to Pippa's? We'll be there in a few minutes, dear. Let Babs know."

I didn't have a chance to argue with my mom or anyone else for that matter because they all hung up. I was ill-prepared to have Luckland's high priestesses in my personal space. It would be an invasion of an army of busybodies. There wasn't enough coffee in the world to get me ready for that. I glanced at a grinning Devon.

"Will you please go and change, so you don't look like someone who spent the night here."

"I don't have spare clothes."

"I thought you kept a bag in your car?"

"Nope."

I was sure he did, but I didn't have time to argue because a knock sounded at the door. Devon went to answer it in his well-worn jeans and sleep-rumpled t-shirt. The ladies marched in one by one. Each of them gave him the once over, then paused at his bare feet. I hung back and gripped my mug with both hands, holding on for dear life.

Devon ushered them all into the living room, where my limited seating quickly filled up.

"Ladies, if you'll indulge me for just a moment, I have a few questions. Just a few, I promise," he said. "As I'm sure you all now know, I work for the FBI. As to why I'm here in Luckland, well, that's a little complicated. I work on cold cases, and I've been chasing the Panellos for their involvement in the theft of money from a Vegas casino." He glanced at me first, then the others, one by one. Seemed he was trying to gauge their expressions. I don't think anyone batted an eyelash. Not even Babs.

"What you may not know is that the Panellos bought four of your shoeboxes at the yard sale, and I want to do a follow-up to get them back. So, I need to know what's in those shoeboxes you're so desperate to find. I know it's not ashes."

My mom glared at me ever so slightly before she turned to Devon. "Devon, honey, we can't tell you exactly. But trust us when we say everything we value is in them. Anyway, it's for your own good that you not know."

"But you asked me to find them."

"Well, yes. You're an FBI agent. Who better?"

"I think Kate is trying to say that we trust you implicitly, and you would return what belongs to us without fuss." Matilda smiled as if that said it all.

"So, you're saying that whatever is in those boxes has nothing to do with the Panellos."

"How can they? We'd never heard of those men until they came to town," Hope said.

"And it wasn't until they pointed a gun at us that we knew they were wicked. We certainly wouldn't associate ourselves with their sort. We're not criminals," Pru declared.

That was debatable, but it seemed the ladies were going to dig their heels in. Time for me to intervene. "Devon. As far as your investigation is concerned, you're in Luckland for the Panellos. The Panellos held us at gunpoint. We don't know why. If you need to mention shoeboxes in your report because you know the Panellos bought them at my mom's yard sale, then simply state it was purely coincidental. The ladies have told you the shoeboxes contain nothing but sentimental items and would like them back. Simple."

Everyone stared at me, and heat flushed my cheeks. I wanted to look away from Devon, but his gaze on mine was a little mesmerizing.

Matilda nodded. "Okay. Devon, I think we all agree with what Pippa said. There will be no mention of shoeboxes on our side, as they are irrelevant. We will reiterate what we told the authorities yesterday, that we have no idea why the Panellos were holding us at gunpoint." What she meant was the discussion was over. Done. I was fine with that. The air had gotten a little thick anyway.

The ladies, including Babs, stood then marched out the door as if nothing had changed, which, for the Luckland Divas, probably hadn't. Life simply went on for them. I wondered how old someone had to be when that sentiment kicked in. My nerves weren't cut out for their kind of deceit. I didn't want to lie to anyone.

Once they'd gone, he turned to me. "That went well."

I smiled. "Thank you for not telling them you knew about the money and the blackmail. Let them keep their secrets."

Devon shook his head. "I've never known anyone to be so stubborn. The four of them together are a formidable force."

I laughed. "Yes, they are. So, what happens now?"

"You give your testimony, and I hope the Panellos incriminate themselves."

I slipped into Devon's arms and gave him a hug. "In the meantime, can you find out what they did with those boxes? That might give us a lead as to who has them."

"Yeah. I can try, but I'm not going to hold my breath."

CHAPTER TWENTY-TWO

LATER THAT AFTERNOON, WE ALL HEADED OVER TO THE SHERIFF'S satellite office. The building was quite small, just big enough for a few desks, a holding cell for those rare occasions when someone committed an actual crime, and a room with a solid, windowless door for interviews. It looked more like a broom closet, and I wouldn't have been surprised if it had been at one time.

Devon waited while we all sat on the few chairs available in a narrow hallway. "Right. You ladies make yourselves comfortable. Another agent and Deputy O'Hara are going to ask you questions. Just...keep it simple." He shook his head, and I admit I felt a little sorry for him. He could no more rat out his mother than I could mine, but his career was on the line if anyone made the connection between the Vegas heist and the millions the ladies had squirreled away.

Slowly, one by one, Babs, then the Luckland Ladies disappeared into the room, only to come out again full of smiles. I was the last one in. I sat on a little hardback chair—the plastic kind like those in grade school.

"Can you state your name?" a man in his mid-thirties asked,

which had to be the FBI agent as I knew Deputy Martin O'Hara, a local to Luckland.

"Pippa O'Leary." I should have known this would be tedious. I just hoped they didn't ask anything too personal. I wasn't sure any of them knew that Devon and I had, though not a relationship, certainly a "thing" going on.

"Ms. O'Leary, why were you at the Panellos' residence yesterday?"

"They hired my sister to redecorate. I was there to help her."

"Are you a decorator?"

"No, I'm a photographer. I was there to photograph the rooms."

"What evidence do you have that they hired your sister?"

I frowned because that question seemed to come out of left field. "She told me they did. Plus, they attended Matilda's party, and everybody discussed it."

"You received a threatening postcard recently, did you not?"

Devon must have told them. "Correct. Did the Panellos confess to sending it to me?"

The FBI agent glanced at his notes but didn't answer me. "You were also the victim of a break-in?"

I sat forward in my chair and rested my arms on the table. "Yes, which I assumed had something to do with the postcard. Is that what you think?"

This time the agent glanced at Deputy O'Hara. "That's something we'll question them about. Right now, we want to know how you and your sister managed to detain one of the gunmen."

"There was only one gun, which Freddie had. We took down Frankie. Babs and I know a few self-defense tricks."

"Yes, you tripped him? What is that move called, out of curiosity?" The agent smirked, and I wondered what it would take to wipe it from his face.

"I wouldn't think it had a name. It's just something my sister and I do."

"Do you do that often?"

"Only when held at gunpoint by a couple of crazy brothers." I hoped the agent didn't have any more stupid questions because I felt incapable of holding in my irritation. After a few heartbeats, the agent nodded slightly.

"So, how did you call Agent Devon Marks for help?"

"He put an app on my phone, you know, in case of emergencies."

"And why would he do that?"

"Because someone broke into my home." I thought the answer was obvious. The agent must have also thought so because he glanced at his notes once more.

"Did the Panellos say anything you might have deemed suspicious?"

"Suspicious, how? The men are raving lunatics holding a bunch of old ladies at gunpoint. I wasn't really listening to them; I was trying to figure a way of keeping them distracted until Devon got there."

The agent nodded again. "Well, thank you, Pippa. We'll contact you if we have any more questions."

Free to go, I scraped the chair back, then hightailed it out of there. As the FBI agent hadn't asked about money, I could only assume the Panellos hadn't mentioned it either. Maybe they weren't so stupid after all.

The hallway was empty except for Devon, who leaned against the wall.

"All done?" He pushed away from the wall and stood next to me.

"Yeah."

"Can I follow you home?"

I didn't see why not. We still had a lot to discuss. I nodded, then smiled. "Coffee and cookies?"

His answering smile eased some of the tension from my shoulders, and when he linked his fingers through mine and led me outside, the rest of my stress dropped away completely.

Once we arrived back at my place, and I'd made us coffee, Devon sprawled on the couch with 99, and I relaxed in my recliner while we munched on raspberry and white chocolate cookies.

"So, Devon. What's next for you?" I figured he'd go back to Quantico or wherever super-secret agents go.

"Not sure, Pip. I'm kind of worried about those boxes and their contents. I don't like that the ladies have secrets in them."

"I don't either, especially as they won't say what they are. I mean, if we knew, we might be able to avoid any repercussions." He must have seen the worry on my face because he put 99 down, then came over and pulled me into his arms, holding me gently.

"We'll find them. I promise." He didn't look so sure, and neither was I. After a moment, he pushed a stray strand of my hair behind my ear. "Hungry?"

Nothing like food to change the subject. I smiled. "Actually, I'm starved."

There weren't a lot of places to choose from in Luckland, so the obvious choice was always going to be the Blue Sky Café. It wasn't very conducive to a private conversation as literally half the town could be found eating there, and with the recent publicity from the lasagna recipe leak, probably the entire State of Colorado.

The other thing about a small-town café was that everyone knew everyone, and the second we walked in, it almost felt like being on a sitcom where the most popular guy walked into the bar. Most of the local diners hadn't seen Devon in years, and they called out in greeting. Their reception made me smile, except for one—Morgan, the town flirt.

Instead of saying hi like most people, she said in her fake little imitation southern accent, "Oh my, look what the wind blew in."

Keep it in your hoop skirt, Scarlet O'Hara.

She even picked up a napkin and fanned herself before she ran up to him and placed her hands on his chest, examining him as though he were some sort of specimen. Had I been with any other guy, I probably wouldn't have cared. I'd have flashed a grin and let them untangle themselves from her—but Devon was another matter, and for the first time in my life, that little green monster reared its exceptionally large and ugly head. I wasn't prepared for such a reaction, which must have shown.

Devon removed Morgan's hands, murmured who knew what to her, then looked at me and smirked. I gave myself a mental shake, and we grabbed a table as far away from Morgan as possible, which wasn't easy since the place was packed.

More people stopped by our table to say hello. It seemed Devon had become a local hero, having saved the Luckland Ladies from the dangerous duo—according to Hope's recitation of events that had traveled like lightning through the town. Eventually, we were able to order something to eat. The latest addition to the café was a wood-fired pizza oven that produced enough heat to kick out an authentic Neapolitan pizza in about two minutes. No question that was what we were going to order.

"Sausage?" I asked him, not even bothering with the menu.

"Ground beef?"

"Not very adventurous of you," I said. "I guess it's halfsies then." Right then, I decided I'd have to work on his pizza choices with him. Leftover *hamburger* pizza wasn't going to work in my fridge.

Though I didn't want to talk about the Panellos, they were still forefront. "What do you think will happen to the Panellos' house?"

"Well, they hadn't purchased the place. They were only renting it."

"Renting? They led everyone to believe they'd bought it. Actually, that's kind of a relief."

"Why?"

"Despite what happened there, I love that house. It's now on my wish list."

"Really? What else is on your list?"

"Hmm. Well, I'd like to start a studio. I'd also love to visit Ireland, as you know." Funny, I hadn't really had a wish list until recent events and after Devon showed up. I guessed, factually speaking, Devon was on my wish list too—but he most certainly didn't need to know that. "What's on your wish list, if you have one?"

"Well, let's see. Athens. A Maserati. And season tickets to the Rockies baseball team."

"Not the Nationals?" I held my breath because the Rockies played in Denver, so season tickets to the Rockies really meant coming home. Here. To Luckland.

He didn't answer. Just grinned and winked. My face immediately heated as he locked gazes with me, and it took some moments before I could look away.

After dinner, we went back to my place, and I sank into a serious case of awkwardness. I sensed Devon was as nervous as me, and I could only assume he was thinking of consequences. We'd known each other for years. Our mothers were best friends. Therefore, a fling was out of the question. If anything were to happen between us, it had to be long-term.

The moonlight slivered through the window and lit up his incredible green-blue eyes. They glittered with desire, and as he leaned in, so did I. A millimeter away from the touch of his lips, he stroked my cheek.

"Red?"

It was a question to make sure I understood what was about to happen, and I only had one answer.

"Yes."

With a groan, Devon pressed his lips to mine, and I snaked my arms around his neck, surrendering in a way I very rarely let myself. Eyes closed, my limbs pliant, I allowed him to pick me up and carry me to my room, his soft murmur a promise in my ear.

The following morning, I awoke alone and instantly felt... empty. I'd never experienced something so profound—not in that way, and I didn't like it one bit. I supposed I expected Devon to still be at my side, but then I remembered the conversation we'd had as he'd held me in his arms and rested his chin on my head.

He'd asked me if he should stay in Luckland, and I'd hesitated before I'd answered. His question wasn't lighthearted, and everything rode on my response. If it were about me, my answer would have been an automatic yes, but it could possibly mean him giving up his career with the FBI if there wasn't room for him in the Denver office. I didn't want him to lose the job he'd obviously worked so hard to get, and I certainly didn't want to be the cause. When I told him exactly that, he'd sighed, and I'd instantly regretted my answer.

I sat up, wishing I had a chance to answer him differently. Last night, I should have realized Devon and I had something far more than a wish. What we had was real, very, very real, and I may have blown it.

Soft purring had me turning my head, and I smiled at the ball of fluff asleep beside me. So, not alone, but not who I wanted to wake up to. As I stroked along 99's fur, I noticed a small package with a bow sitting on Devon's pillow.

His pillow.

Pushing that thought aside, I eyed the note with "Open Me" written in a large scrawl.

Curious, I pulled the ribbon. Inside the box was an incredibly beautiful locket, and judging by the amount of tarnish, quite old. Was this his purchase from the yard sale? I gently took it out and opened the clasp. I honestly didn't know what I'd find. There on the left was Devon in his lab coat and goggles. On the right was a photo of me in my feathered hat holding a snare drum.

"Whaddya say, Red?" Devon stood in the doorway. Not with his usual cockiness though. He seemed to be waiting with his head tipped in that way he had. Making my heart melt.

"You're staying?" I hardly managed to ask the question because my throat felt tight.

"Affirmative." He smiled. I smiled back, though my pulse raced as if I were about to plunge off a cliff. What if he *couldn't* stay? What if, after a day or two, or a week, or a month, things went south? I tightened my fingers around the locket, unable to fight the niggle of doubt that wormed its way into my heart.

"What about your job? I mean, I know Denver has an FBI office, but what if they don't have an opening?"

"We'll figure something out, Red. There are other options, you know."

I wasn't so sure, but down to the very core of my soul, I wanted to believe him.

CHAPTER TWENTY-THREE

I HAD BARELY STARTED COFFEE WHEN THERE WAS A KNOCK ON THE door. I froze, glancing at Devon, who seemed unconcerned about a visitor so early in the morning.

"It's them," I whispered. "Don't let them in." Though I'd dressed, I felt vulnerable because I hadn't yet had my caffeine fix. I really wasn't ready to face the ladies, no matter what they were here for. Devon, however, didn't seem to have the same compunctions. He grinned and headed to the front door. I followed a few steps behind.

"Good morning, Pippa," my mother said as she walked in. Tilting her head slightly, she smiled. Not the *nice to see you* kind of smile either, but the *I know what you've been up to* smile.

The others, including Babs, followed suit, single file, each with the same smug smile. Not one of them said a word to Devon. They all beamed at him. That was when I realized they all knew—every one of them. My face must have flushed a bright red because Devon leaned in close to me.

"They were going to find out sooner or later," he said.

"I was rather it was later. Much, much later."

"So, why do you think they're here?"

"I don't know, but I guess we're going to find out." We headed into the living room, where the ladies had once again filled up all the available seating except my recliner. Devon appropriated it, and 99 jumped up onto his lap.

With no other choice, I stood next to the recliner. "Can I ask why you're here?"

Matilda smiled. "Well, it's about Devon. After what's happened, we all feel Devon might decide not to go back to Virginia. Are we right?"

I glanced at Hope, wondering if she'd had Marcy use her Tarot cards again.

"It's something Pippa and I have discussed," Devon said.

"Shall we assume you would like to continue with the FBI?" my mom asked.

"That's safe to say, Kate," he replied.

"But not necessarily a deal-breaker?" Hope asked.

"No, not a deal-breaker." He laughed at that.

Matilda grinned. "Then it's settled. You'll stay in Colorado, and if the FBI refuses to have you, you can have your investigative agency. You'll be a real gumshoe!"

Devon looked skeptical. Or horrified. "I appreciate what you're suggesting. However, I'm not sure Luckland has enough mysteries to solve. Though I did hear yesterday that Lillie Stanton thinks she has a ghost in her attic." He chuckled and waited for everyone else to laugh as well. Nobody did.

Wanting to save him any embarrassment, I leaned close so only he could hear. "You forget, around here, rebellious spirits and hauntings are serious business." Once upon a time, I'd have considered it the ultimate victory to make him squirm, but now...

He looked up at me and smiled. "Thanks, Red, duly noted."

I smiled back, relaxing for the first time since the Luckland Ladies had invaded my home. Again.

Devon faced the rest of the room and cleared his throat. "Look, I want to earn enough to support myself, and someday, I hope to have a family. *Someday.*"

I wasn't sure if he'd directed his remark at me, but if he included me in that *someday*, I'd take it.

The ladies all started babbling excitedly, and Babs put her thumbs up. I couldn't help but grin even though Devon and I hadn't discussed the future.

"Ladies," Devon said over the noise. "I'm only going to ask this once. Is there anything at all about the business with the Panellos that might prohibit me from being a thoroughly ethical agent for the federal government? Think carefully before answering."

That shut everyone up.

If I still had a wall clock, I would have heard it ticking; the silence was so thick. Devon sighed.

"I suppose I'd better start thinking of a name for this new company of mine, am I right?"

As abruptly as it stopped, the chatter started right up again, with the ladies shouting various names they felt would be appropriate for the new spy agency in town. As the ladies began commenting on how nice everything was turning out, Devon stood and handed 99 over to me.

"All right. We can adjourn this little impromptu meeting. What do you say?" He looked around at everyone expectantly, but nobody paid any attention; they simply continued to chat away.

I shook my head and did the only thing that worked in those situations. I let loose my whistle. "I believe Devon is saying everybody needs to go home now," I said nicely. "Or go shopping. Go to lunch. Go wherever you like—but *go.*"

After the last one filed out, still chatting, and Devon had shut the door behind them, he chuckled. "Seems as if I need to practice that. Otherwise, they are going to trample all over me. I've been away too long."

"So, you're going to resign?"

"I have to. With everything I know, I couldn't work for the FBI and do so without compromising my integrity, and I couldn't put the ladies through an investigation."

I could understand Devon's dilemma, but it proved where his loyalties lay—with family. "What are you going to tell your bosses?"

"Well, I'm going to be honest and say that having my family and those I love"—he placed a hand on my cheek—"terrorized by the criminals I was pursuing has made me realize I was putting everyone in danger."

I leaned into his touch even though I felt bad for him. He seemed to love his job, and the idea of him giving it up for me, well, for all of us, was a lot to handle. Nevertheless, he was staying, and we were now an item. I'd already invested my heart, so I had to accept that things were changing. I wondered, though, if he'd be truly happy.

"Don't worry," he said as if he could read my thoughts. "Life has a way of righting itself."

CHAPTER TWENTY-FOUR

Over the next few days, I spent most of my time taking as many photos as possible of the spring foliage because springtime was short in Colorado. As long as I had a gallery of fabulous photos, I could take my time with the blog posts.

By Friday, I was ready for my kick-back night, with Devon for company. We'd decided on a nice quiet dinner, followed by a movie, and we were just heading over to the café when his phone rang. The instrumental version of "Waltzing Matilda." Devon definitely had an odd sense of humor. I idly wondered what ringtone he'd chosen for me when he hit the Bluetooth speaker button.

"Devon, my boy, is Pippa with you?" Matilda asked.

"I'm here, Tillie."

"Fabulous. Would you two mind popping by for just a short visit if you aren't terribly busy?" The phrase *terribly busy* didn't leave much room for excuses, and Devon put the blinker on and turned off to her house before I could even answer.

I sighed. "Be right there, but only for a few minutes, okay?" I honestly doubted we'd be allowed to leave after a few minutes, but after Devon hung up, he squeezed my fingers.

"Don't worry. I'll make sure we're out in time for dinner."

Grateful, I was about to smile when I saw all the cars outside Matilda's house. The women could literally walk to one another's houses, but to have driven there... "Oh, no. Now what? Do you know what's going on?"

"Not a clue."

We climbed out of the car, and from the glance Devon gave me, it seemed he didn't like this any more than I did. I held my breath as we headed into the house—until I saw the huge banner in the front hall.

"Welcome Home Devon!"

"Are you freaking kidding me?" They were throwing him a party. Well, truthfully, that wasn't what annoyed me. Not one of them bothered to clue me in. As Devon's girlfriend, significant other, or partner in adventure, I would have thought they'd include me in the party planning.

As they all yelled, "surprise," I froze with my hands on my hips. Devon looked at me as if he knew I was ready to blow a fuse. "Easy, Red."

I couldn't let my aversion to surprises ruin his celebration. I'd learned to deal with little surprises, like the locket, which was a sweet surprise, but since Devon's return, it seemed as if my life had been one big surprise after another. At that rate, I'd need a pacemaker. I smiled apologetically at Devon and forced myself to relax.

Devon worked the room. He was seriously good at that. What was awkward nerdiness in his youth had become charming, and he most definitely wore it well.

When I noticed him having an animated conversation with Tom, it gave me pause. My brother-in-law wasn't the lively conversation type unless it was work-related. He *would* talk your ear off if the topic was historical preservation or the rise and fall of mid-century modern, so seeing them chatting away made me curious. If I waited, I could probably corner Tom and weasel some information out of him. I *could* wait a little longer and just ask Devon, but I already knew I'd get nothing out of him. Babs, though, would tell me.

Determined to solve that particular mystery, I grabbed a couple of glasses and a bottle of cabernet, then nudged Babs to follow me. We headed outside and sat on the steps that led off the deck, away from prying eyes.

"Okay, Babs, what's with Tom and Devon? I haven't seen Tom that enthusiastic about party chitchat since the time Prudence brought that home and garden producer to the town's Founders' Day."

"No. I'm not going to discuss this with you. Anyway, I have no idea." She damn well did. I could tell. Desperate to find out, I played the guilt card I'd saved for just such a moment.

"Babs, remember when Mom and Dad went to the cabin, and you borrowed the car? Remember that? Remember the little incident you had? I had to bribe Tommy Thistle to fix it before they came back. Meaning I had to go out with him. On a date. You said someday you'd pay me back. Consider it someday." I knew I had her then. She was nothing if not loyal about paying her debts.

"Okay, but only if you come over this weekend and help me paint Leah's room."

"You just painted it last month," I replied.

"Those washable markers you gave her? Not washable." She then took out her phone and showed me her daughter's first masterpiece. I must admit it was stunning.

"Deal."

"You didn't hear it from me."

"Hear what?" Devon asked out of the blue.

Are you kidding? How does he do that? I shook my head in frustration.

"Oh, Devon, there you are! I think Tillie is looking for you," Babs said quite smoothly. Like Mom, Babs was quite a natural when it came to thorny situations.

"Nice try, Babs." At least Devon had the good grace to laugh since he was ruining a perfectly good confession. Babs, of course, looked totally relieved as she put down her glass and raced off, deserting me.

Devon immediately sat. "What is it you want to know, Red," he asked. He picked up the empty wine glass and refilled it.

"Well, Sherlock, I'd like to know what you and Tom could possibly have to talk about."

"No can do, Watson. Highly confidential."

His reply was as I expected, but as soon as I opened my mouth to try and wear him down, he kissed me. As with every other kiss he gave me, it went all the way to my toes and did the desired effect—it shut me up. Devon pulled back, then grinned before he went back inside. Damn it all. Eventually, he'd tell me. *If* I lasted that long.

Once the party ended, Devon and I had a short but necessary conversation on the way back to my home. *My* home because, while he was sort of bunking at my place, he hadn't technically moved in.

"Pip, I know you aren't too keen on surprises. I get that, but they meant well."

"I know. I just need to expect the unexpected, eh?"

He laughed and squeezed my hand. "You have to admit; life will never be ordinary for us. I suppose I should keep that in mind."

I had no idea what he meant, but I hoped he was saying he wouldn't ever throw me a surprise party.

The next day turned out to be quite eventful, in a very Luckland way. Devon received a phone call from the sheriff, who explained the Panello brothers had pleaded guilty to holding us hostage by gunpoint. They told the sheriff they'd arrived home to find all of us had broken in. Fearing we were going to rob them, they held a gun on us. It was a ridiculous story, and the authorities had agreed.

Sitting out on the back porch on my swing, enjoying an unseasonably warm night under the stars, I turned to Devon. "So, they didn't confess to trashing my house or sending the postcard?"

"No, which isn't surprising, but I have no doubt they were responsible. The Vegas sign on the postcard is too much of a coincidence, and I don't believe in coincidences. Most likely, they were looking for the money and believed the women owned the house, which as you know, they do."

"So, what happens now? Will the Panellos go to jail?"

"They will, but I don't know for how long. I'm kind of out of the loop now. I only know what the sheriff told me."

"And what about the Vegas heist? Any luck on getting them for that?"

"Unfortunately not. The trail has run cold. They were smart until they came to Luckland. At least they *will* be going to jail."

It wasn't exactly what I'd hoped for, but it was better than nothing.

"What about the shoeboxes? Did they tell you what they did with them?" I asked.

"Actually, yes. They said they never opened them and handed them off to a couple as they were leaving. They'd only bought the boxes to avoid drawing attention to themselves."

I almost smiled at that because, with the getups they wore, those two men would draw attention to themselves no matter what they did. "Did they say who the couple were or what they looked like?"

"No. That's where we draw a blank, which brings us back to square one." He sighed. "Don't worry, we'll find them." He pulled me close and locked his gaze on mine, totally distracting me from the subject of crimes and misdemeanors.

***

A week later, Devon had another surprise for me—a romantic candlelit dinner, and I thought it the perfect time to talk to him about what he was going to do about starting his investigating firm.

"You know, Devon, about your PI business. If you decide to go ahead and start one, I am one hundred percent in. Finding those shoeboxes can be our first case, then we'll need to figure out who is threatening the ladies with their secrets."

Devon smiled—aa sexy smile that confirmed how much I wanted to be with him.

"I'm glad you're all in, but before we get started, I'll need an office of some sort. Preferably a home office. Somewhere to hang my hat."

"Well, what does Tom say? I know you've been discussing this with him." I smirked to remind him, no secrets. Why Babs couldn't have told me, I had no clue. I'd had to drag it out of Leah, for goodness' sake.

Devon smiled. "He's got a few homes that might be of inter-est. I told him I was looking for something special to put my stamp on. Something with a few projects to tackle."

"Projects? What, are you on an episode of House Hunters now?" I really couldn't see it. Picturing Devon with a toolbelt, though quite appealing, didn't seem to match up with what I knew of him.

"No, but I'll keep it in mind. I just think I can tackle a few things if it saves on the cost of setting up everything."

"Ever remove wallpaper? Ever shingle a roof? Ever even been on a roof?" I asked, pretty sure he hadn't.

"No, no, and yes, actually. Remember when you used to lay out by the lake at the cabin, and when you thought nobody was around, you'd go topless?"

Okay, enough of that line of questioning. The idea that when my seventeen-year-old self was removing tan lines, his seventeen-year-old self was up on the roof, watching, was not something I wanted to think about.

"Future reference, Kemosabe, some things are meant to remain secret."

He grinned. "Duly noted, Red."

Ordinarily, with our new relationship status, we would have gone off together for a little...dessert, but the incessant buzzing of our phones signaled it wasn't going to happen.

Mom: Come quick. Café. Another leak!

Another leak? I looked at Devon, but he seemed as confused as me.

When we got to the café, we learned that someone had leaked Hope and Marcy's cheesecake recipe, which was far worse than the lasagna. Their cheesecake was practically perfect. It could be made sugar-free and gluten-free and still be amazing.

"I don't understand what's going on," Marcy said. "Why would someone leak our recipes, and how did they get them?"

"Were they in the shoeboxes?" I asked, hoping that might make the ladies admit to what the boxes contained. "If so, whoever has them might be leaking the recipes, though that doesn't answer why."

Hope frowned. "Oh, you're right. Those recipes were in the boxes."

Marcy nodded in agreement.

I grinned. Now we were getting somewhere. "So, our priority is still to find the boxes and stop the recipe leaks." I would also have loved to mention the threats they'd received, but they still didn't know Devon knew. The ladies all glanced at one another, and I wondered if they were thinking what I wasn't saying.

"There is more in those boxes than just recipes. It's imperative we get them back. Preferably before Founders' Day," Matilda said.

I frowned. "What's so important about Founders' Day, other than the obvious?"

"Never you mind. Just, please get those boxes back."

The next few hours were spent at the café over a few slices of cheesecake while we all pondered why the Blue Sky recipes were suddenly going viral. If whoever had the boxes, whether the four the Panellos handed over or the other two from the yard sale, was leaking the recipes, the question was why. Nobody had any logical answers.

CHAPTER TWENTY-FIVE

"Yoo-hoo!"

"Anyone home?"

"Pippa, come open the door!"

"Devon, are you there? Your car is here. I assume you are too."

Devon graciously opened the door and let in the cyclone.

"Wonderful news, children," announced Prudence as they all marched in.

"Just splendid, really," said Hope.

"I am so excited for you!" exclaimed Marcy.

"Serendipity, that's what it is," declared Matilda.

"Pippa, you're going to love this," my mother said.

All of which terrified me. When these ladies behaved that way, they'd done something that clearly couldn't be undone. I wondered if Devon realized it. I glanced at him.

"Well, since you're all here, please, sit." Before I'd even gotten the words out, they'd all sat down. I tried not to let on that barging in on a new couple's morning wasn't quite the most appropriate thing to do. As if they cared.

"Coffee, anyone?" Devon asked, which I thought was quite considerate of him.

"At a time like this? No time for that now, my boy," said Matilda.

"Guess who called this morning, Pippa?" Mom asked. Not waiting for a reply, she kept going. "Letisha, and she told us the Tindle place was for sale. Well, I immediately called the girls."

I didn't think Devon knew Letisha was the local realtor, but I figured he'd catch on.

"Seems the family was planning on auctioning it, but we put a stop to that, by golly," Prudence said, her tone emphatic.

"Please tell me you didn't buy it, did you?" I had to put a stop to the torture they were inflicting on us.

"Of course we did, Pippa," said Matilda. "You love that house. We all know it. And it's perfect for Devon's new PI firm."

I looked at Devon to see how he was handling the news. By his clenched jaw, he wasn't.

"*First*, maybe now would be a good time to let you all know I won't be opening a PI firm anytime soon. The mayor and the town council decided they would like their own police force here in Luckland, and they offered me the job of police chief."

"Well, isn't that nice, Devon!" Matilda remarked. She didn't seem surprised.

"Splendid, dear," said Prudence.

"And did you take the offer?" asked Hope, though she appeared to know the answer already.

Devon glanced at me. "Yes, I did, but *second*—I can buy my own house, thank you."

I stared at him because he'd never mentioned the job offer to me, and I was rightly miffed. What had me clenching my own jaw, though, was that Devon didn't seem to want the house and intended to turn the gift down just because the ladies bought it. I had to say something because I *did* want that house.

"Devon, why don't you bring in that pitcher of tea? In fact, I'll help you." I pulled him out of the chair and tugged his arm to keep him moving with me. "Okay, Devon, what's wrong?" I whispered as soon as I got him into the kitchen.

"I'm more than capable of buying my own house. I don't need them to do it."

"Listen, Scooby, it's what they do. You know that. You need a house, and they buy it. Welcome to Luckland. Anyway, they didn't just buy *you* a house. They said they bought *us* the Tindle place because they knew it was a house *I* loved. Is that the problem? Did they assume too much about us? Because if that's what's got you acting like a kangaroo turd, don't worry. I still have my own place, and I don't need to step foot into yours. You take the manor house." I turned my back on him and headed back to the living room. Nirvana never lasted.

Devon followed after me, a pitcher of tea in hand. Once he'd served everyone, they immediately continued to chatter about the house and his new job. Devon didn't seem to realize a town our size wouldn't typically have a budget for a police force, not without a generous benefactor, which meant the interfering ladies probably set it up—a fact that would annoy Devon if he knew. So, it seemed his only issue was with the house, but he'd obviously forgotten they were just being who they were—people who took care of their own, which he was throwing in their faces, and mine.

When I lost my temper, it wasn't a pretty sight, so rather than risk a rather ugly scene, I stewed in silence and waited for them to leave. In the meantime, I changed my mind and decided *I* would take the house, and Devon could simply take over my lease and live in the craftsman. Once the ladies had signed all the paperwork, I could pack up and move to *my* new home. Well, once it had a fresh coat of paint, the roof repairs were made, and the kitchen redone. I might need Babs and Tom to do the honors of renovating and decorating it, but eventually, I would move in. Not Devon.

Finally, the ladies left. I swore it felt more like twenty years than twenty minutes. As Devon showed them out, I headed to the garden to devise all the ways I would torture him—and to stop the waterworks. I was mad, yes, but at the same time, my heart had cracked in two. If Devon wasn't with me for the long haul, my worst nightmare would have come true. I'd have gambled my heart and lost.

I heard him behind me, and I put up my hand to stop him as Matilda had done. It didn't work. I'd have to practice that move.

"Peace offering," he said, holding out a fresh cup of coffee. Then he handed over a croissant, which admittedly did soften me up a bit.

"Ready to listen now?" he asked in that voice that would melt an iceberg. Reaching over, he gently swiped a tear off my cheek. "I made you cry. I'm sorry for that. I promise you, here and now, I will try my best never to do that again. Ever." He sighed and tipped his head, a soft smile playing on his lips. "I should be allowed one mistake, right?"

"I've counted at least three major errors in the last hour alone, but perhaps I can make an exception just this once, but your excuse better be good." I wanted to establish from the outset that I was the redhead in this relationship, and histori- cally and genetically, having a bit of a hothead reaction was reserved for me.

"First things first," he said. He kissed me. Long and slow. "Okay. That should hold you for a minute while I do the talking. I was going to tell you about the job, I swear. I was waiting for the right moment, but the ladies forced my hand. You have to agree becoming the town's police chief is quite the perfect opportunity. I stay in law enforcement and get to stay with you too. Win-win." He kissed me again for good measure.

"As for the house. Well, *I* wanted to buy it. I was going to fix it up. The way you always imagined it. That was what all that talking with Tom was about. Then I was going to, you know, surprise you." He grinned at that last bit.

"You were going to surprise me? Do you have a death wish?"

"I just might, Red. I just might."

"So now we fix it up together, you get to live to surprise me another day, and I get my dream home? As I see it, it's all good, Double D."

"Double D?" he asked.

I smiled because I'd stumped him that time. "Dashing Devon."

That landed me right back in another light-up-the-sky lip-lock.

"Tell you what, Ranger Red, let's go inside. I'll make crêpes." That was all he needed to say. Now the tiny little bump in the road was all settled, life could return to normal in Luckland. Except, of course, I had to make sure Devon didn't figure out how he ended up being the new police chief. We also had to find those boxes and figure out who was threatening the posse.

It seemed *normal* in Luckland was just the calm before the storm because it wasn't long before I got another dreaded text.

Babs: Come to Pru's. EMERGENCY.

SNEAK PEEK AT THE NEXT
LUCKLAND MYSTERY
ALIENS AND THE DEARLY DEPARTED

CHAPTER ONE

BABS: COME TO PRU'S. EMERGENCY.

Babs was my twin sister, and she was serious. Or seriously itching for trouble. I sighed and got out of bed, then tripped over 99, my feline ball of white fur. With only one eye barely open, I looked for a pair of shorts and a t-shirt, preferably clean, and prayed there would be coffee waiting for me when I got downstairs. That was one of the fabulous things I'd begun to discover about having a significant other. While I battled with my tangled-up mane of red curls, Devon dressed and made me coffee. I didn't have to say a word—he just knew, for which I was extremely grateful.

Fifteen minutes later, I was out the door, heading over to Pru's, coffee, laptop, and camera in hand, with Devon by my side. I looked at him and marveled over what had brought us together. Having grown up with him as the literal boy next door, he'd been more of an annoyance than anything else. Then he'd left for college. When he'd recently returned to help us find some missing shoeboxes, he'd pretended to be a private detective, which naturally led me to see him in a different light. I smiled as I remembered how angry I'd been when I found out that instead of him being Magnum PI, he was FBI, which took some getting used to. Not as much as getting used to the fact his Aunt Matilda had turned out to be his mother. That was going to take a lot longer to digest.

On the short drive to Pru's house, I wondered what on earth might have happened to her. My first thought was that she'd fallen down the stairs. She liked to tip the bottle a bit, so her having a fall wasn't all that far-fetched. My second thought was basically no different than my first, though it had her falling off the scaffolding that surrounded her house.

"Do you think she's conscious? Maybe she broke a hip? Old people do that, you know."

"Easy, Red," Devon said.

Though my real name was Pippa, he called me Red, a left-over from childhood. There was a time, not long ago, I would have elbowed him for it, or worse. Not anymore.

"She's not that old, and I'm sure it's nothing like that, we would have heard the ambulance, and of course, I would have heard the call."

Point taken. As Luckland's new chief of police, Devon would have received some sort of notification that one of his citizens needed help, especially when said citizen was one of the four matriarchs of the town, who, coincidentally, were our mothers and their lifelong friends.

"Okay, Colonel Mustard, what's your theory?" I was still a little new to the whole investigation thing. When I thought Devon was a private investigator, I'd gotten the idea I might also like to be one. Even though Devon wasn't a PI, there was no reason why I couldn't learn from him, so I considered myself in training.

"My theory, Pippa, is that we have no idea what's happened, and so for now, we'll wait and see." He chuckled as he said it. He thought my jumping to conclusions was charming. Or so he said. I sighed. His answer was really no help at all. He was lucky he was more than hot, or I might not have let it go so easily.

We pulled up and parked in front of Pru's brick colonial, which would have blended right in if we were in, say, Virginia—in the woods somewhere...with a lot of fog. Her house had always been unusual for the Eastern Slope of the Rocky Mountains. Homes here tended to be built from wood and stone and were quite Victorian with their gables and wide inviting verandas.

Stepping through the open front door, we found the posse already gathered in the kitchen. The women had been friends since childhood. Inseparable. Matilda, Devon's former aunt and now his mom, wore a strange sari-like garment. She smelled like incense and wove her hands in the air while holding a bunch of twigs. Hope, who was the calm in the center of the storm, primly sat at the kitchen table, stiff as a board yet totally put together, as always. Over at the kitchen counter, Hope's fiancée Marcy arranged a tantalizing platter of breakfast treats. They owned a café, so the food was expected. My mom fluttered around the table, literally wringing her hands and pacing in different directions while muttering to herself. My sister Barbara, Babs—as we knew and loved her—stood by the door with her husband Tom, both looking as if they were ready to bolt at any second. The only person missing was Prudence Smalley herself. Definitely not a good sign.

Between my mom's muttering, Tillie's chanting, and Babs firing questions at Tom, it was chaotic.

"Ladies, Tom, if you'll all just give me your attention for a moment?" Devon asked, trying to instill calm and order. Nothing happened. He tried again. Again, nothing. I felt it was time for me to intervene. My dad taught me to whistle. Not the *whistle a happy tune* kind of whistle. The other kind. I put my pinky and index fingers in my mouth and let out a shrieking sound.

Success. The blissful sound of silence.

"Duly noted, Red. Thanks." Devon really appreciated my assistance in keeping the posse in check. "Now then, who wants to fill me in?" he asked.

Everyone began talking at once. I could have reminded him that the first rule when dealing with these ladies was to direct questions to one woman at a time. Addressing the group had been an open invitation to further chaos. I waited to see how he would manage this one. He looked at me, his eyes a silent plea, but I tended to lose focus with those baby blue greens flashing at me. I smiled and shrugged. To be effective as the new police chief, he'd have to master the essential skill of commanding the room.

Curious, I watched as he snatched up the tray of rolls and pastries from the kitchen counter, then headed to the table with it. It was a shrewd move because the cacophony suddenly died as everyone concentrated on picking their favorite.

"Well done," I said softly, so nobody else heard. I liked to give credit where it was due. Plus, it earned me a wink and a grin.

"Let's try this again," he said as he turned to my mom. "Kate? Can you tell me what's happening? Where is Prudence?"

"I'd be happy to, Devon." My mother always liked to be selected first. Though she hid it well, she had a competitive streak.

"I came by here this morning on my way to the store to pick up an old flask Pru wanted to sell." By store, she meant our family antique business, which she and my dad started years ago. "When I arrived, she wasn't here."

"What time was this?" Devon asked.

"Seven fifteen sharp."

"Perhaps she went to town? Maybe a brisk walk? Did you call her cell?"

"Don't you think we thought of all that?" My mom sounded offended.

Matilda jumped in at that point. "Oh no, Devon. When I was talking to Pru on the phone this morning, she said Kate was at the door. Then she hung up."

"What time was that, exactly?" Devon asked.

"Seven precisely," said Matilda.

"I see, and because Kate just said she came over at seven fifteen, it couldn't have been her at the door when Pru hung up," Devon said, stating the obvious, but then he asked a question that didn't have an easy explanation. "Mom, can I ask what you're waving around the room?"

"I saw this on a ghost-hunting show. It cleanses the home. Removes evil spirits," Matilda replied, very matter-of-factly, as if she'd done it before. I was pretty sure she hadn't.

"Aah," he said. "A smudge stick. Don't you need to burn it for it to work?"

"Only if you don't possess natural powers of your own, my dear." She said that as if it were an ordinary statement. "Don't forget, there is a special energy in Luckland. That's why Native Americans used to live on this land. The energy helped their special blend of elemental and earth magic. That energy also increases our abilities."

Devon and I exchanged a quick glance. I pursed my lips to keep from reacting. Devon did the same.

"How did you all get in here anyway?" he asked the others in the room, which I assumed was to change the subject. He should have learned earlier, but no. They all started talking at once.

"Door was open," said Matilda.

"Hope let me in," said Babs.

"Tillie let me in," said Hope.

"I came in through the back milk door," said my mom.

Devon turned to her. "Milk door?"

"Yes, of course, dear. Years ago, the milkman brought the milk in those lovely glass bottles and would come to pick up the empties. Houses like this have milk doors so the milkmen could come in and leave the milk in the mudroom." She could have just said the back door, but not simplifying anything was typical of my mom.

I leaned toward Devon and whispered, "You know they all have keys." I assumed he'd forgotten, considering he'd been away from Luckland and the ladies a long time.

Devon sighed. "Has anyone searched the house? Maybe she's here somewhere."

"But of course. How silly do you think we are," said Matilda. "I came running over as soon as Kate called. We searched the house together, then we called Hope, who texted Babs, who texted Pip."

There were a few things wrong with that. First of all, Matilda didn't run. Ever. As far as searching the house, I had my doubts. They probably just stood in the foyer and called out to Pru. I wasn't going to say anything, however. I wanted to see how Devon would handle it.

"Unfortunately, unless there are signs of foul play, I can't put in a missing person's report for twenty-four hours." He checked his watch. "It's only been forty-five minutes. I will, however, take a look around. I want everyone to stay put in this room, please. Don't touch anything. Just remain here. I'll be back in a few minutes."

I followed him into the hallway, but he stopped me from going farther. "Wait with the others."

"Excuse me, Encyclopedia Brown, but perhaps two heads are better than one?" I was referencing a book he used to carry in his back pocket when we were young. He was always pulling it out and reciting things.

"Might be so, Pip, but as your newly appointed police chief, I'm gonna have to go solo on this. Besides, I need you to keep an eye on everyone."

I knew that last part was just to placate me, but I allowed it because I was, in fact, quite concerned about Pru's disappearance. Though that didn't change, it fell onto the back burner when the house shook after a thunderous boom from the basement.

CHAPTER TWO

It was so quiet I could hear a pin drop. We lay on the floor, Devon completely covering me. I didn't know how that happened except I remembered him literally grabbing me like we were in a scene from an action thriller movie.

"Everyone okay? Pip?" Devon asked, his tone hushed.

"I will be, I'm sure. Right now, I'm feeling a little squashed," I said, assuming he'd get up. When he didn't move, I nudged him. "Hey, Andre, I could use a breather here." Devon was a lot larger than me—tall, broad, muscular with the kind of rock-hard abs I used to just read about.

He rolled off, none too gently, and had stood before I could even pull myself to a sitting position. I'd have to get him to teach me that.

"Stay. Don't move," he said as he headed back into the kitchen. I could hear them all in there, so I had to assume everyone was okay. No blood-curdling screams indicated dead bodies, so I didn't panic. Yet. I did wonder how long I was supposed to stay, however. Patience wasn't my forte, especially when I almost had my body blown into little, tiny bits. I wasn't exactly obedient, either. While I did take his request under advisement, there was no way I'd just sit there. I stood, gave myself a once over to ensure I still had all my limbs, then headed back into the kitchen.

"What part of don't move didn't you understand, Pip?" Devon shook his head in wonder, or perhaps annoyance, at my small act of rebellion. It wasn't the first time I'd not obeyed his *orders*. I was quite sure he knew it wouldn't be the last.

I didn't respond—too busy double-checking on everyone's well-being, which was a force of habit. As a photographer, I was accustomed to reading the room and getting a take on situations, and after a recent turn of events that had thrust me into the heart of mystery and mortal danger, I constantly tried to hone my investigative skills.

"Maybe we should look downstairs?" I asked, knowing full well the reaction I'd get.

"Maybe you should let me handle this." Devon gave me what I fondly referred to as the melting look. Meaning he directed his crystal blue-green eyes right into mine and tipped his head slightly. No woman could resist, and it melted me all the way down to my toes. I guessed we were at a stalemate. I really wanted to see what had happened. What if Pru were down there? What if she'd accidentally blown up the furnace? The possibilities were endless, and I took a few deep breaths to relax.

"Pippa, dear, let Devon do his job. Why don't you sit? Have a bagel," Hope said, no doubt trying to be the peacemaker.

"Yes, dear," said my mother. "Sit down and eat while Devon takes care of this."

"Try the rhubarb cream cheese. It's wonderful," Matilda said.

God, we were all recovering from a near-death experience

after an explosion in the basement, and they wanted me to sit and eat. I'd have thought any normal person would suggest we get out of the house and run like hell.

"Everyone, please, if you'll indulge me for a moment, I need you all to carefully, very carefully and quickly, make your way outside. Now. We could have a gas leak."

I knew Devon would be the voice of reason. I smiled, but of course, the rest of them all started talking at once, leaving me to settle it with another whistle.

"Okay, everyone, out. Now. Unless you have a death wish." That seemed to work. If nothing else, Devon needed to keep me as his sidekick to ensure cooperation in situations like that. The kitchen emptied pretty speedily, everyone filing out the front door and down to the street. Devon must have used his new handy dandy radio to call the sheriff's office as I could already hear sirens. Clearly, we had an emergency requiring additional assistance.

"You too, Pip. Get yourself across the street with the others, then get as far away as possible."

"And leave you here? Oh, no can do, Kemosabe," I said. I meant it too. Our romance was too new for me to see him blown to bits. If he were in danger, I'd be right there with him.

"There's a pizza with extra sausage in it if you do," he told me. "You also get to pick the movie Friday night."

"Anything I want?"

"Anything you want. Now go."

Devon appeared to be a fast learner. My weaknesses were food and sappy movies that ended with me ugly crying. So, I headed over to the group huddled at the end of the driveway, then rounded them up to cross the street. Not that I thought that offered any real protection, but if it made Devon feel better, I could give in once in a while.

The first fire truck pulled up, accompanied by several sheriff's vehicles and the gas company's truck. Martin O'Hara, one of the deputies, pulled up in front of us. He lowered his window and leaned across the console.

"Morning, ladies," he said, tipping his hat.

"Good morning, Martin. Have you come about the bomb?" my mom asked.

"I've come to see what's what, and until we know, I'm afraid you ladies will need to head back to town. We're going to need to evacuate the area," he said.

I braced for the reaction he was going to get. I was not disappointed.

"Oh, my no, Deputy. We can't go anywhere. We must find Prudence first," said Matilda.

"Yes, you see, she's the reason we're here, and what if she's trapped in there?" asked my mother.

"Officer Marty, I'm sure you realize we can all be of assistance if we stay here," said Hope using their familiar name for him.

"Ladies, please, you'll have to leave and quickly. This is a dangerous situation. There could be another explosion," he explained—patiently, I might add.

Hope shook her head. "Don't worry. We don't mind being blown to smithereens."

That pretty much summed up our little group. I waited to see how the deputy would respond. Trying to corral these incredibly stubborn women who had no qualms about standing their ground wasn't easy. My money was on charm, which was about all they responded to. He looked like he'd been around the block a time or two, so I hoped he had a snappy comeback.

"Ladies, I appreciate your devotion to Miss Prudence. We all want to find her safe and sound, and if you truly want to help us do that, we need you to put your heads together and help us come up with some ideas. I think there's no better way to do that than over some of your delicious fresh Danish pastries at the café. What do you say? You can even ride in my car, and I'll turn the lights on for you."

Not quite snappy, but very effective. Thus, Babs and I walked back to the Blue Sky Café that Hope and Marcy owned while everyone else piled into the patrol car. I was pretty sure no seat belts were involved. We arrived before they did, which told me they somehow took a few detours along the way.

We pushed a couple of tables together so we could sit and discuss the current events, and we invited the deputy to stay and have a Danish with us. I had a feeling he would have stayed, either way, ready with some questions.

The deputy's approach was very different from Devon's. If Devon had been there, he'd have started firing off questions immediately. All business. Martin O'Hara just sat back and let them all talk. His approach was something I'd have to consider. If I were to become a first-rate investigator, I needed to learn various techniques. Maybe the fact Martin grew up alongside our informal women's club and graduated high school with them called for a distinctive style. Once we were all away from the scene of the crime, as it were, the ladies addressed him far less formally. He was simply Marty.

I eventually got a little impatient. I needed some updates.

"Do you know anything more? Can you find out what they know?" I asked him point blank. "Maybe you can ask Devon for an update." I could have asked Devon myself, of course, but I assumed he was busy investigating.

"These things take time, Pippa," he said.

"What if Pru doesn't have any time?" No sooner had I asked than I realized I'd probably stepped over some invisible line. Fear turned his face a few shades paler. From his reaction, I would have said he had a thing for Pru. Perhaps his concern was more than professional. With my curiosity peaked, I would have loved to know more. However, there was no time to ponder Prudence and Martin's relationship as we really, really needed to find her.

THE LUCKLAND MYSTERY SERIES

Grande Dames and a Vegas Heist
Aliens and the Dearly Departed
Mislaid Love and Found Bodies
Stolen Recipes and a Dead Chef
Vengeful Spirits and a Lost Gold Mine

More to come!